SWORD OF PROPHECY

Heroes of Asgard Book Three

S.M. SCHMITZ

MYTHOLOGY GLOSSARY

If Gavyn gives one of the characters a nickname, I've put it in parentheses right after his or her actual name

Adonis—one of Aphrodite's lovers, Adonis is the Greek mortal known for his beauty. The myth begins, though, with some really messed up incest, which results in Adonis's mother being turned into a tree...and that's how she gave birth to him. Somehow. Y'all, I don't know. Mythology is totally disturbing sometimes.

Aesir—one of the two tribes of gods in Norse mythology, and the tribe associated with most of the Norse gods such as Odin, Thor, and Tyr. The other tribe is the Vanir.

Anhur—Egyptian god of war who was sometimes portrayed with the head of a lion, which is why he can shift into a lion in this series.

Anubis—in Egyptian mythology, Anubis is a god of the dead and is associated with jackals.

Arnbjorg—isn't a real mythological figure; I made her up for this story. She is the love interest of Havard.

Asalluhi—Mesopotamian god of incantations and magic.

Asgard—the realm of the Aesir, one of the two races of gods in Norse mythology. The other is the Vanir (who originally lived in Vanaheim).

Baba Yaga—in Slavic mythology, Baba Yaga is a supernatural witch-like being, who lives in a hut on chicken legs. Yeah, really.

Badb (Agnes)—Irish goddess of war. One of the triune of goddesses who form the Morrigna.

Belatu-Cadros—Celtic god of war. His name is also given as Belatucadros.

Dagr—in Norse mythology, Dagr is the personification of day. Odin gave him a horse (Skinfaxi), and he and his mother, Nótt (night), would ride around the world bringing day and night.

Ekimmu—Sumerian vengeful spirits.

Enki—Sumerian god of magic and wisdom, and father of Marduk and Asalluhi. His Babylonian counterpart, Ea, was regarded as the creator and protector of humanity. Because he's associated with Ninhursag in Sumerian myths, they are married in this story.

Forseti—in Norse mythology, he is a god of justice. The only mention of him in the *Poetic Edda* discusses his home and identifies him as someone who settles disputes. I've made him the mediator in this series as well.

Frey—Norse god of prosperity, fertility, and peace. He and his sister, Freyja, are members of the Vanir and were brought to Asgard to live among the Aesir when the war between the two tribes ended.

Freyja—Norse goddess of love, sex, fertility, and war. Known for her unparalleled beauty, she's often coveted by different gods and mythological figures, while she tends to covet jewelry, particularly Brísingamen (her necklace).

Gerd—gastroesophageal reflux disease. Just making sure you're paying attention. In Norse mythology, she's Frey's wife. Frey saw her from a distance and instantly fell in love with her.

Goibniu—in Irish mythology, Goibniu is the smith and is often associated with brewing, which is why he's also the bartender in Murias.

Gunnr (Keira)—a Valkyrie. In Norse mythology, Valkyries would select which men would fall in battle and bring them to Valhalla.

Havard—isn't a real mythological figure. He's made up for this story, in which he's a god of war. I know his name is a pain in the ass (trust me: I'm the one who's having to type it), but I chose it because of its meaning. It contains old Norse elements that translate as "high defender" and I thought that was fitting for his character. If it helps, I keep pronouncing it as "Hav-ard."

Hecate—Greek goddess of magic, witchcraft, the night, the moon, and necromancy. I would *not* mess with her.

Heimdall—Norse god whose impeccable sight and hearing make him an excellent watchman for the unfolding of Ragnarok. He also possesses the gift of foresight (ability to foretell future events).

Hildr (Heidi)—one of the Valkyries.

Idun—Norse goddess whose apples grant the gods eternal youth.

Inanna—Sumerian goddess of beauty, love, sex, war, and justice. Yeah, I have no idea why the ancient Sumerians decided to lump all those different characteristics together. Maybe they just ran out of deities.

Inti—in Incan mythology, Inti is a sun god and was one of the most important deities of the Incan civilization.

Jenny Greenteeth—an English witch who drowned people in a river.

Ljósálfar—in Norse mythology, it is the realm of the "light elves." In this series, it refers to the Norse's name for Ireland.

Mama Pacha—in Incan mythology, Mama Pacha is an earth and fertility goddess who can cause earthquakes.

Marduk—patron god of Babylon, he is a complex figure associated with magic and incantations, and is often syncretized with Enki and Asalluhi.

Medeina—a Lithuanian goddess of forests who is sometimes depicted as a she-wolf with an escort of wolves...so, of course, she can take the form of a wolf in this series.

Morrigna—a triune of Irish war goddesses formed the Morrigna. The three goddesses are usually given as Badb, Macha, and Nemain, although Nemain is sometimes replaced with Morrigan or Anand. Each goddess represents a different aspect of war.

Nergal—ancient Mesopotamian god of war and pestilence who commands a number of demonic entities.

Ninhursag—Sumerian mother goddess who is regarded as a creator of gods and men. She is the mother of Ninurta. Seriously, these family trees are complicated as hell, and Gavyn is more than a little suspicious that this whole war is just a family feud gone nuclear.

Ninurta—another ancient Mesopotamian war god, Ninurta played a small enough role in *The Unbreakable Sword* series to warrant a bigger part in this series. His enchanted weapon, Sharur (sometimes a talking mace, sometimes a talking spear) will be back in book two, but unfortunately, it doesn't talk to Gavyn.

Njord and Skadi—I reference their ill-fated marriage, so here's the gist of the story: Skadi lived in the highest mountain where the snow never melted, and Njord lived on the beach. They loved their homes, and since those homes were completely different, they were miserable whenever they stayed with their spouse. Eventually, they decided to return to their homes separately since neither could be happy in the other's land.

Nótt—personification of night in Norse mythology. She rides a horse across the sky, which drags night behind her.

Nuada—in Irish mythology, Nuada is the leader of the Tuatha Dé who is a great warrior and ruler but loses his right arm in a vicious battle. Since a blemished king couldn't rule, he was forced to give up his throne. The god of healing, Dian Cécht, made Nuada a silver arm but it wasn't enough to get him the throne back, so Dian Cécht's son, Miach, causes skin to grow over the silver appendage, which pisses off his dad because he was all like, "How dare you show me up!" so he kills him. *Kills* him, y'all.

Odin—the All-Father of the Aesir, Odin is one of the most famous gods of Norse mythology. Although he's a war god, Odin is also associated with magic and wisdom. His wife is the goddess, Frigg.

Paricia—an obscure name in Incan mythology, this god may be synonymous with Pacha Kamaq. He is most known for sending a flood to wipe out people who weren't paying him the proper respect. In this series, he is a water deity since he's sent tidal waves to punish people for not submitting.

Ra (Most Loathsome God in the Universe)—in Egyptian mythology, Ra is one of the sun gods (specifically, god of the noon sun). He is associated with falcons and is often depicted with the head of a falcon.

Róta—one of the Valkyries.

Serpopard—an animal found in Mesopotamian and Egyptian mythology, it's supposed to be half leopard, half snake.

Sharur—Ninurta's enchanted weapon (either a mace or spear), which could supposedly talk…I'm really not sure what good a talking weapon is.

Sif—in Norse mythology, Sif is Thor's wife. An earth goddess, she is best known for her beautiful blond hair, which Loki infamously cut off as a prank…and not surprisingly, Thor didn't take it too well and threatened to kill him. Loki got away with his life after promising Thor he'd have a golden…wig?…made for her. The same dwarfs who make Sif's new hair make Mjollnir as well as several other gifts for the gods.

Supay—in Incan mythology, this god of death rules over Ukhu Pacha (the underworld) and commands an army of demons. Gavyn is not a fan.

Thor—god of thunder, storms, and fertility, Thor probably shares the top-honor of being the most recognizable Norse god along with his father, Odin. He defends Asgard with his hammer, Mjölnir, and is also known for being a protector of humans.

Tiamat—Babylonian goddess who takes the form of a dragon to battle Marduk. She's just a dragon in this story and not a very nice one.

Tuatha Dé—the gods of Irish mythology. Also known as the

Tuatha Dé Danaan, which means "tribe of (the goddess) Danu."

Tyr—Norse god of war who lost his right hand when he put it in a wolf's (Fenrir's) mouth so he could be restrained. So look: Fenrir would only allow himself to be restrained if some dumbass stuck a hand in his mouth because he suspected the fetter the gods had brought was enchanted. And Tyr was apparently that dumbass. I mean, the gods *did* bind the wolf that was prophesied to be such a terror, and *supposedly* he's gonna stay bound until Ragnarok just like his dad, Loki (yeah, because Norse mythology is F.R.E.A.K.Y y'all), but he'll just break free then and kill Odin anyway, so what was the point?

Ull—Norse god associated with archery. Not much is known about him, but it's always good to have expert archers on your side.

Valaskjalf—one of Odin's halls. While Valhalla is the hall associated with his dead warriors, Valaskjalf is where he watches over all the realms.

Valhalla—one of Odin's halls. Famously portrayed as having a golden roof, slain warriors are brought to Valhalla by Odin's Valkyries. Here, they fight each day in preparation for Ragnarok and those who fall again rise each night when they all dine with Odin himself. Peachy afterlife, huh?

Vanir—one of the two tribes of Norse gods, the other being the Aesir. Frey and Freyja are from the Vanir.

Vigrid—field on which many battles of Ragnarok are prophesied to occur.

Yngvarr—doesn't exist in Norse mythology; I made him up for this story. Brother of Havard and also a god of war.

Zababa—ancient Mesopotamian war god.

CHAPTER ONE

What's worse: facing an entire supernatural army, a poison-filled dragon, or a hostile labyrinth of horrors? Oh, wait. We were facing all three.

The illusions within the maze-like building made escaping from it all the more difficult, because when faced with an entire supernatural army, a poison-filled dragon, and a hostile labyrinth of horrors, we *needed* to make our journey home more difficult. Agnes, as confident as ever, led us through winding hallways and stairs that *seemed* to be going up, but we never actually got back to the ground floor and somehow, only ended up on the exact same floor where we'd found Frey.

After our third attempt of going up the stairs and finding ourselves back at square one, we decided to look for alternate ways out of the building, partly because I'd declared war on those stairs and stabbed a few of them with my sword. Not surprisingly, the stairs didn't seem to care and still refused to let us go back to the ground floor. But for good measure, Joachim shot an arrow at them before we walked away, and Tyr hurled a number of colorful insults in their direction, but I guessed the stairs didn't speak English.

"Any chance you speak Sumerian?" I asked.

Tyr shook his head and tried some Norse profanity, but the stairs must not have spoken Norse either.

Frey glanced between us and said, "How exactly did *this* group manage to find me?"

I was about to tell him, "With my impeccable leadership and fighting abilities," but Agnes beat me to it, so I scowled at her instead.

"What if I break a hole in the wall?" Thor suggested.

"Aren't we below ground?" I asked. "Can you tunnel out of here?"

Thor stroked his beard for a moment as he thought about it then shrugged. "It's a better idea than walking in circles and trying to kill a staircase."

"An *evil* staircase," I muttered.

"Try not to open a huge hole in the wall," Agnes said. "Start small in case there's something dangerous on the other side... this place isn't like Asgard, so we shouldn't assume it's dirt and rocks below their ground."

Even though I was desperate to get out of this building, I began to have serious reservations about Thor's plan. As much as I hated it when Agnes was right, there could be something far more dangerous than evil staircases on the other side of this wall. I had flashbacks to scarabs attacking a metal door so violently the damn thing dented and burst open. And worse, mutant devil dogs with human features and the ability to whisper to one another... in *English*, which I thought was kinda weird, but then again, I'd never encountered mutant devil dogs before so what did I know about their language preferences?

I stayed back as the giant god approached the wall and carefully lifted Mjollnir then tapped the wall like he was a sculptor working with expensive marble. Chunks of wall fell to the floor anyway, and even though I didn't want to find out what it felt like to have my head smashed in by a hammer, my mouth betrayed me anyway. "*Man*, I feel sorry for Sif."

Thor glanced over his shoulder at me. "Mjollnir is enchanted, Gavyn. It's powerful enough to break through mountains."

I nodded like I'd already known that and had just been messing with him. "So what's behind the wall?"

Thor peeked into the hole he'd created and tapped his hammer a few more times then turned toward us. "Good news or bad news first?"

We all groaned and backed farther away from Thor *and* the wall. "Good first," I decided. "Because if it's not *really* good news, I can always go back to Frey's prison and just lock myself in there."

"How?" Frey asked. "The locks are on the outside of the door."

"Would you not point out the flaws in my plans?" I snapped.

"Would you both shut up?" Agnes also snapped, but she was really snapping at me.

"Okay," Thor said slowly. "Good news is that I *can* break through the wall. The bad news is that it appears to lead to another room."

"Another room," we repeated just as slowly.

"And it's kinda dark, so I can't really see what's inside that room."

"Nope," I said. "I'm out."

"Just going to stay in this dungeon forever?" Joachim asked.

"There are no devil dogs or homicidal beetles in here," I said. I cringed as soon as the words left my mouth, because I'd stupidly forgotten that in this world, words had the magical ability to produce freakish, nightmarish monsters that wanted to kill us. And go figure, no sooner had I closed my mouth than the buzzing of wings and hard shells hitting doors and walls responded, as if telling me, "Hey, dumbass, you called us?"

"Um," Joachim said, "should I even ask what that is?"

"Possessed beetles. But what exactly *kills* possessed beetles?" I said.

"Why are they possessed?" Joachim asked.

"They're trying to kill us," I pointed out. "Pretty sure that's not normal beetle behavior."

Joachim nodded thoughtfully and said, "Our track record with possession isn't that great."

"You know," Agnes said, "I don't normally play along with your idiocy, but I'll make an exception for possessed beetles."

I pointed my sword at her and nodded. "But it would be great if you'd finally become useful. I mean, what's the point in having a witch as an ally if none of her spells work?"

The hard bodies of all those scarabs beat against the door, and their wings buzzed louder like they were pushing against it, attempting to bring it down and pour into the room. Thor cleared his throat and said, "Yeah, I'm going to break this wall down now."

"That's probably a better idea than trying to exorcize demon beetles," I agreed.

"Again, our track record with exorcisms isn't so great either," Joachim said.

Agnes and I nodded as Thor swung his hammer at the wall, causing a deep hole that led into a dark room. Now, I'd never claimed to be a physics expert, but it seemed like the light should spill from our room into the dark one, allowing us to at least see if it was empty. But even though the hole was big enough to walk through, the room remained as dark as if it were still completely sealed.

Behind us, the scarabs beat against the door and the hinges began to creak as the door bulged against their weight. I groaned and squinted into the dark room—not that it actually helped me see what horrors awaited us in there but just because it pissed me off that our choices were flesh-eating devil beetles or a room so terrifying, even the light didn't want to enter.

Thor stepped aside and grinned at me. "After you."

"Can't," I lied. "I have a rare disease that prevents me from entering rooms that will likely result in my death."

"Screw it," Frey sighed. "I've already been taken their prisoner. I'll go."

"Good idea," I started to tell him, but those damn beetles broke through the door and began flooding our room. Tyr, who'd been closest to the door, screamed as some of the oily-black scarabs landed on him, his prosthetic hand slapping wildly at his bloody skin. Thor immediately darted across the room, surprisingly fast for a giant of a man, and grabbed Tyr's arm, partly pulling and partly dragging his friend with him toward the mystery room. Instead of sending Frey into that dark room alone, we all hurried in even though we had no way of keeping the scarabs out.

But the weirdest thing happened when I stepped into the total darkness of the secret room. Blindingly bright light burst out of every corner, forcing me to shut my eyes or risk permanent cornea damage. And it apparently didn't only affect gods and demigods. Those beetles, which had clearly escaped from *The Mummy*, made this gods-awful shrieking noise and refused to follow us. I reached out to find my friends and feel my way around the room and I made contact with *something*, but Thor grunted at me and ordered, "Let go of my ass, Gavyn."

So naturally, I smiled in the direction of his voice even

though everyone else most likely had their eyes closed, too. "That's not what you told me last night."

"Dude," Joachim said. "Don't make me take my chances with the beetles."

"Anyone else get bitten by them?" Tyr asked. "Think I'm going to turn into a scarab-pire now?"

"Probably," I told him.

"We all know who I'm biting first then," Tyr muttered.

I wasn't even going to pretend like I didn't deserve that.

"Find a wall," Agnes instructed. "Thor can break open another doorway for us."

"Marco Polo," I suggested. "Only Thor should move until he's found a wall then we'll follow his voice until we reach him."

"That's actually a good idea," Agnes said.

"You don't have to sound so surprised," I shot back, but really, I'd surprised myself, too.

We waited silently as Thor shuffled around looking for a wall. Occasionally, the demon beetles forgot the light seemed to burn them and they'd attempt to enter again only to make that unholy shrieking sound. I didn't even know beetles *could* make a shrieking sound, but clearly, these weren't normal beetles.

Thor finally found a wall on the opposite side of the room from where we'd entered and guided us toward him as he broke another hole in the wall. We'd have to hope whatever awaited us on the other side wasn't too dangerous because we couldn't open our eyes to check it out first.

I followed my friends into a new space and tried to open my eyes, but even there, I couldn't see. The world seemed completely dark, but gradually, I sensed movement, and as I blinked, trying to clear my vision, I finally figured out where we were.

Somehow, we'd ended up *outside* even though I was pretty sure we'd still been in the basement of the building. But now, we were standing on the lawn near the front entrance. And we'd been surrounded by an entire army of Sumerian gods and heroes.

CHAPTER TWO

Over the past few weeks, I'd been finding myself in some pretty shitty situations, but vision impaired and surrounded by an entire supernatural army had to be the worst of them. Because fighting my way out of a tough situation wasn't the problem: having to do it while my eyes tried to adjust from a near-blinding experience was a *huge* problem.

"Agnes," I whispered. "Any chance you know a spell for restoring eyesight?"

"I'm not really a witch, dumbass," she snapped.

I shrugged because isn't that what an incognito witch would say? But I didn't have time to argue with her about it. A shadowy figure—probably a man or woman and not one of Supay's demons considering I'd already killed that bastard—emerged from the side of a building. My occasionally, or always, sluggish brain realized there must be a door there, and that's where all of these soldiers were coming from.

Since I was at least temporarily near-sighted, the Sumerians were nothing more than vague, colorless shapes. Worse, my peripheral vision and depth perception were completely messed up, meaning I couldn't exactly tell how far our enemies were from us. But I noticed Agnes had closed her eyes again, her sword raised and ready, and she seemed to be concentrating on something. I wanted to ask her what the hell she was doing, but my heart leapt into my throat instead. Because one of those shadowy figures charged her, and while she was close enough for me to at least sort of see her clearly, she was too far away for me to help her.

Joachim was shooting arrows at whatever spilled from the doorway of the building in front of us, so Agnes had no one to save her... and she just *stood* there with her eyes closed. The once murky shape revealed itself as a rather large man with a sword, and he attacked my witch, but my mouth fell open when she somehow parried and forced a bit of distance between them. The man regained his footing and attacked again, but Agnes once again knew he was coming and deflected a second time.

I thought about yelling, "You said you weren't a witch!" but she still seemed to be concentrating and I didn't want to distract her. But I wasn't so stupid I didn't know how she was defending herself, even with impaired vision. There was clearly a reason she had the reputation of being one of the most badass warriors among gods: Agnes was using sound to fight. Besides, I had my own problems to deal with, like the abnormally giant guy who lunged at me, swinging *something* at my head.

I swung back, the blade of my sword making contact with whatever this Cyclops was trying to kill me with. The damn thing *roared* at me—the Cyclops, not his mace or bat or hell, I didn't really care what kind of weapon he had—which convinced me I wasn't fighting a man but yet another monster, but I never had the chance to find out what he was. A screech from above warned us the poisonous dragon was returning.

"Gavyn," Tyr yelled. "We need to find cover!"

I swung at the mystery monster again, but completely missed, which made him laugh. At least, I assumed he laughed. I wasn't really sure *what* that sound was supposed to be, other than a disturbing cross between a moan and a cackle. I felt the heat before my wounded eyes could see the fire erupting from the dragon's mouth. Part of me wondered where the fire actually came from, but a bigger part of me wondered why the hell my dumbass was still standing around waiting to get barbecued.

Frey grabbed my arm and pulled me away from the flames. We stumbled as we ran, and as Frey fell, I tripped on his legs and fell forward, too. The dragon screeched, like the bastard was laughing at us along with the Cyclops, so I cursed them both but especially the dragon since it was about to roast Frey and me. I mean, that wasn't how I was supposed to die, and being burned alive was *definitely* unacceptable.

But nothing in this world ever made sense, and the dragon was no exception. Frey and I were helpless on the ground, yet the dragon screeched one last time then suddenly turned around, flying away from us.

"What the hell?" I muttered.

Those shadowy figures in the distance had gotten closer so that they formed distinct shapes and colors. Unlike the dragon, they weren't mysteriously retreating, and if Frey and I didn't get to our feet soon, we'd die anyway.

Agnes appeared out of nowhere—or maybe she'd been catching up to us the whole time but I'd been too preoccupied with almost being flame broiled to notice—and shot an arrow into some guy's heart who'd been about to shoot an arrow into mine. I scrambled to my feet just as two more guys behind the dead one took aim at us.

"Agnes, would you turn them to frogs already?" I shouted.

"For the last time, I'm not a witch," she shouted back.

Tyr finally caught up to us, and with my vision clearing, I

could see just how badly those scarabs had injured him. He'd lost a lot of blood, and he'd paled considerably. He seemed to be concentrating on just staying on his feet. Thor walked beside him, throwing Mjollnir methodically to keep threats away from his injured friend, but we had to get out of this city and get Tyr medical help.

Joachim joined Agnes in unleashing a volley of arrows at our attackers, but an escape seemed impossible. We were outnumbered with a badly injured god and inside a labyrinth. And apparently, the only opening in the veil was outside this city's walls.

I backed against a building so I'd only have to worry about attacks from one direction, but I'd just steeled myself for about a dozen sword fights when a woman's voice whispered, "Take this orb and throw it at your attackers."

A slender hand reached out of the building—not out a window or door but the actual wall of the building, because *that* wasn't terrifying at all—and held out a small orb with dancing shades of a faintly glowing blue. And naturally, my first thought was to hack off the weird arm extending from a building and trying to get me to take a mysterious crystal ball. My second thought was to tell Agnes another member of her coven had shown up, but she was still shooting arrows at the demigods attacking us.

And since we were all about to die anyway, my *third* thought was, "*What the hell.*" I grabbed the orb and threw it at the horde of heroes, which by the way, turned out to be a lot more than a host.

The orb shattered as it hit the ground, and that blue light from within erupted, passing through the army that had been pursuing us. As the light hit them, they froze, sometimes in mid-step, and even the arrows they'd been shooting back at us became suspended in the air. Agnes, Supernatural Witch

Numero Uno, lowered her bow and stared, dumbfounded, at the statuesque demigod horde.

That same creepy arm emerged from the wall again, accompanied by the woman's voice that said, "Fifty feet to your left is a hidden door. I'll signal you when you've reached it."

And since the bodiless arm *had* given me a magical orb that had paralyzed all the assholes trying to kill me, I started walking. But she sighed loudly and snapped her fingers to get my attention. "Your *other* left, dumbass." This time, she pointed in the direction she wanted me to go for good measure, so even though I was taking directions from a single arm jutting from the side of a building, I grinned sheepishly at it and turned around.

Our battered rescue party cautiously approached this secret doorway, and while I'd seen countless impossible things in this city, I was still surprised when the wall rippled and a doorway appeared with a pretty brunette standing in it. And not just her arm either but the entire goddess. So naturally, I thought the wall must be some sort of an illusion, and I tried to put my hand through it but only managed to jam a finger.

The goddess glanced between my hand and my face and said, "Are you seriously the hero we're counting on to save the world?"

"No," I answered. "I'm pretty sure I'm just here for comedic relief."

She nodded in what I assumed was very real agreement and stood aside so we could enter the building. "Hurry," she instructed. "Asalluhi is nearby."

As soon as I stepped inside, I noticed she wasn't alone. A man in a pinstripe suit stood by a desk against the wall, and I immediately tensed, sensing we'd been tricked. But the god held up a hand and quickly assured me, "We aren't going to harm you or your friends, Gavyn. We've come to help you escape."

"The dragon," I said. "You made it leave."

He nodded as the goddess closed the secret door behind us, and despite this guy's insistence they intended to help us escape, being closed in that room with two Sumerian gods made me nervous. *Really* nervous. "Who are you?" I asked.

"My name is Enki," he said. "And this is my wife—"

"Ninhursag," Agnes breathed, her eyes widening but aside from Ninhursag being a truly terrible name, I had no idea why it concerned her.

"Um, is she another witch or something?" I asked. I mean, sure, I'd already decided this mystery goddess must be a witch after the whole arm through the wall thing, but I hadn't expected Agnes to agree with me. But she shook her head anyway.

"No," Agnes said. "This is Ninurta's mother."

Okay, I'd been prepared to hear all sorts of crazy explanations, anything from "She's the world's *first* witch" to "These are really lions taking the form of gods in some kind of cosmic rebalancing of nature." What I *hadn't* been prepared for was learning the mother of the god who was leading the Sumerian war on Earth planned to help his enemies escape, including the hero who'd almost killed her son. But maybe she hadn't heard about that, so I wisely decided to keep my mouth shut.

Wait. We all know by now that's not really possible. Let me try again.

I wisely decided to *try* to keep my mouth shut.

"So," Joachim said carefully, "I'm guessing Ninurta's grounded?"

I snorted and Agnes shot *me* a "Shut up before you get us killed" glare even though I hadn't made the joke. In her defense, it had probably just become a reflex by now.

"If he survives," Ninhursag said, "he will most certainly have to be dealt with somehow." She sounded so sad about it I actually felt kinda bad for laughing at Joachim's joke. When fighting gods, it was easy to forget they had families and people who loved them just like we humans did.

Agnes lifted an eyebrow at Ninhursag and said, "Why are you helping us? Aren't you and Enki at the head of your pantheon? And can't you do something to get your gods under control? And Enki, aren't you Asalluhi's *father*?"

I squinted at her and tried to send telepathic messages along the lines of "Lay off the accusations before they smite us" and "Be honest: did you and Yngvarr ever do it while you were pretending to be a million years old?" but apparently, she wasn't telepathic either.

Enki finally moved away from the desk, waving a hand at the wall behind him. Another secret door opened and he shot Agnes a sympathetic smile. "My stepson has grown too powerful and has too many allies for us to stop him on our own," he explained. "We tried to reason with him, and it didn't end well. As for Asalluhi, he forged his own path a long time ago. We haven't exactly been on good terms in centuries."

"Where does that door lead?" I asked. If I ever got out of this city, I was never stepping foot in a magical labyrinth again. Or really, any kind of labyrinth, magical or not.

"To a tunnel that will bring us back to a street that will eventually get us to the city's wall," Enki replied.

"And are there any monsters in this tunnel?" I pressed. "Because my shoulder *just* healed after a couple of monsters tried to rip it off."

"There are monsters all over this realm," Ninhursag answered. "And not all of them will obey our commands like Tiamat."

"Tiamat," I repeated. What the bloody hell was a tiamat?

I smiled stupidly at myself since Hunter had insisted I shouldn't say "bloody hell" and was tempted to say it aloud just to spite him, even though he was in the Otherworld and I was trapped in some Sumerian hell.

"The dragon," Agnes said, giving me a strange look as if she knew what was going on in my head and was thinking, "Still such an idiot," like that was ever going to change.

"The spell that's keeping those heroes frozen isn't permanent," Ninhursag said. "We should probably be going now."

I glanced through the doorway then at Agnes. "Ladies first."

Agnes narrowed her eyes at me and said, "Remind me again why we're friends."

"Because you showed up at my door and kidnapped me, which I'm still kinda pissed off about, to be honest."

"Right," she sighed. "My mistake."

I threw my hands up and cried, "I've been telling you that for weeks!"

"Any chance we can get out of Sumer II before Tyr dies?" Thor barked.

"Sumer II?" I asked back.

"Sumer the Sequel?" he suggested.

"Sumer the Remake?" Agnes also suggested.

Enki and Ninhursag grunted at us and threatened to leave us *all* behind, except for Tyr who really did need to get to a doctor. Thor helped him into the tunnel, and we carefully followed. I'd expected darkness, so I was pleasantly surprised when the walls of the tunnel emitted a soft light, allowing us to see but not blinding us like the hidden room. I allowed myself to hope the rest of our journey would be relatively easy and immediately chastised myself for that thought. After all, that nosy little bastard here in Sumer II who kept plucking ideas from my head had me cornered now, and there was no way he'd let this opportunity pass.

And go figure: no sooner had I finished calling myself a dumbass than a familiar white mist drifted from the ceiling ahead of us.

Enki froze and shouted, "Nerve gas! Go back!"

But as we turned to retreat, more of the milky gas spilled from that direction as well, trapping us inside the tunnel.

Thor shouted and cursed as the toxic gas touched his skin, but to the giant god's credit, he still tried to protect his injured friend with his own body.

"Mjollnir," I yelled. "Thor break us out of here."

"What if there's an entire cloud of this gas behind the walls?" Agnes asked.

"Does it matter?" I argued. "We know it's in here, and we have to do *something*."

Thor nodded in agreement and lifted his hammer, which had proven to be pretty useful so far, even though I'd always thought a hammer was an awfully stupid weapon. His arms had blistered from the gas, but he managed to swing Mjollnir with enough force to knock open a sizeable hole that led into another tunnel.

"Where does this one go?" Agnes asked Ninhursag.

"To a part of Sumer II that we *don't* want to end up in," she replied.

I groaned because what could possibly be worse than a tidal wave alley, a labyrinthine building, a poison-filled dragon, and a demigod army? Then I groaned *again* when I realized I was *still* a world-class dumbass for not learning yet to control my thoughts. But the hair-raising, most frightening sound I'd ever heard had already told me what horrors awaited us now.

The devil dogs were back.

CHAPTER THREE

"Death," one whispered. "Eat," hissed another. And between all their whispers that made *me* want to whisper back, "Just kill me now," were the barks and snarls of those freakish monsters.

"Oh, come *on*," I complained. "It's like the hotel in Chicago all over again."

"Except we're also stuck in a labyrinth," Agnes added.

"And I'm here now," Frey also added. "And wondering what the hell happened in Chicago, because so far, I've gotta say... I'm not a fan."

"It gets better," I sighed. I gestured to the bend in the tunnel where the mutants would round the corner any second now, and if he thought flesh-eating beetles and toxic nerve gas were bad, he'd just *love* these devil dogs: the Sumerians had saved the worst for last.

Sharp claws ticked against the smooth tunnel floor, and misshapen bodies slammed into each other as they skidded and slid and sort-of barked, sort-of whispered something that might have been, "Go to Hell," but honestly, by that point, I wasn't really listening. I was too busy trying to hide behind

Enki in the hopes the devil dogs wouldn't eat him, or at the very least, would save him for last.

"Um," Frey stammered, "next time someone kidnaps me, don't rescue me."

I nodded in complete agreement, and the largest mutt *smiled* at us as he lunged toward Thor, who remained at the front of our group. He knocked him to the ground with his hammer, but another grotesque canine had been right behind the first and jumped at the giant god of thunder before he could get Mjollnir ready to strike this monster down, too. The second dog latched onto Thor's blistered arm, and the Norse god screamed in pain. Screaming usually activated those unbelievably annoying demigod genes that would eventually get me killed, and this time was no exception. I charged the stupid dog with its stupid, vaguely humanoid face. And the stupid devil dog's stupid pack tried to jump *over* Thor to get to me.

Thor's hammer was in his right hand, which just happened to be attached to the arm a particularly annoying dog was using as a chew toy, so he was using his left fist to pummel the beast but it wouldn't let go. It *still* wouldn't let go even after I ran my sword through its side, so I yanked my blade free and decapitated the bastard while Agnes and Joachim fired arrow after arrow into the swarm of insanely disturbing creatures.

But naturally, monsters *this* disgustingly horrifying couldn't be killed by anything as convenient as an arrow, or even a dozen arrows. They continued to snarl and whisper, somehow at the same time, and I'd occasionally pick out words, mostly to the effect of dying and eating. But my wild slashing at the devil dogs was interrupted when I distinctly heard them whispering my name.

"Dude!" I yelled. "That is *not* cool!"

Fortunately, my friends weren't as easily distracted, and I

only managed not to have my throat ripped out because they stabbed the dog that leapt at my face. I looked around the angry swarm of sort-of human, sort-of dog faces and shouted, "Which one of you said my name? Because I'm coming for you next."

I really should've known better, because my threat only made them *all* take up that part-growl, part-hiss of "Gavyn," "Gavyn," "Gavyn." And if you've never had a pack of devil dogs all hissing your name, you might not understand just how seriously I considered taking my chances with the poisonous gas.

"You just had to piss them off, didn't you?" Agnes scolded.

"They started it," I mumbled.

Frey stabbed another demonic canine and glanced over his shoulder at me. "Not to sound ungrateful or anything, but really... next time, just let my kidnappers kill me."

"I have an idea," Thor shouted. "Everybody back up!"

We had no problem complying with his request since it got us farther from those dogs. Even with his arms blistered and raw, and one pretty badly mangled from the razor sharp teeth of these canine bastards, Thor was able to grip Mjollnir tightly and lift it above his head before smashing it into the polished concrete floor.

Cracks formed in response, spreading up the walls and even the ceiling, and half of the surviving devil dogs stumbled and tripped on the broken floor. Thor struck the ground again, and a hole opened between the pack and us.

I was more than a little curious as to whether or not this hole led to the actual Hell and if these Hellhounds would jump in to go home, but they backed away from it, their disturbingly human eyes fixed on Thor. I expected them to start whispering *his* name, but they just growled at him, which was totally unfair.

"What's below us?" Frey asked the Sumerians.

"Water," Enki said, and he sounded excited about that, which I thought was kind of bizarre. So what if we were standing above an underground river? Also appropriate, by the way, since Hades supposedly has all those rivers. But when the water burst from the hole like a Sumerian Old Faithful, I stopped wondering why Enki would be so happy about standing on a water source.

The geyser suddenly changed directions, hitting the devil dogs with enough force to wash them out of our section of the tunnel. They yelped and hissed, "Die!" angrily, but as we'd already learned, there was no point in trying to fight a tidal wave. But, not surprisingly, that also made me question if he'd had anything to do with our near drowning, and being me, I just asked.

"No," he assured me. "I'm not the only god who can control water. But given the way that wave vanished at the end of the alleyway, it was probably Asalluhi's doing."

"Asshole," I corrected.

Enki risked looking away from his own tidal wave to blink at me, so I shrugged. "Well, he is."

The Hellhounds, which I'd decided was a better name than devil dogs, even if Hellhounds were supposedly entirely different, still yelped and whisper-barked, "Assholes!" back at us—okay, maybe not that last part, but I'm pretty sure that's what they were thinking—but they were getting farther away as the water carried them through the tunnels. When we could no longer hear them, Enki allowed the water to drain back into the abyss below us. By now, Tyr was barely conscious, and Frey and Thor were holding him up, urging him to hang on just a little longer.

Admittedly, I panicked a little. Tyr was the first person I'd come to like after being abducted from my apartment, and sure, I was still a little convinced I must be suffering from Stockholm Syndrome, but there was a greater chance I considered Tyr a friend simply because he was a genuinely likeable person.

Enki and Ninhursag led us carefully around the crater, which turned out to be a feat worthy of Cirque du Soleil considering we had a semi-conscious god the size of a VW Bug to get across a ledge that was maybe a foot wide. I forbade myself from thinking as we continued our trek underground, and sure, it probably seemed like I *always* forbade myself from thinking but this time, it was more than usual. We couldn't afford any more delays, and we definitely couldn't risk Thor getting injured worse than he already was. I doubted we'd be able to carry Tyr without him, and we sure as hell couldn't carry Thor out of here.

Sumer II played tricks on my mind again though. By the time Ninhursag pointed out a ladder leading up to a hatch on the ceiling, I was torn between thinking—yeah, I wasn't supposed to be doing that but it's ridiculously hard not to think at *all*—we'd been in this tunnel for almost a day and barely an hour. When I asked Agnes about it, she wasn't sure either. Time had no meaning in this place.

"I'll go up first," Ninhursag offered. "We couldn't go to the street closest to the wall since they clearly know we're down here. Once we're above ground, we still have several blocks to go, and we'll have to be quick."

She reached into her satchel and produced glowing blue orbs, just like the one she'd given me to paralyze the hero horde. "I only have five left," she continued, "so we have to make them count."

"How long will the effect last?" Joachim asked.

"Normally, about half an hour, but Asalluhi is tricking us, making even time seem like an illusion. We can't count on our senses to judge how much time has passed."

"Man, I hate that guy," I muttered.

Although to be honest, if I were going to have supernatural powers, being a god of magic would be the way to go.

Ninhursag placed an orb in my hand and told me not to drop it, so I squinted at her and said, "You didn't tell anyone else not to drop it."

"Gavyn," Agnes sighed, so I turned to squint at *her* now and tell her I was an idiot, not a klutz. And the damn thing may or may not have slipped from my fingers. But if it *did*, my lightning fast reflexes—or Agnes's—allowed me—or Agnes—to catch it before it shattered on the ground and paralyzed us all. And if all of *that* actually happened, Ninhursag would have most likely arched an eyebrow at me and crossed her arms as if to say, "And that's why I said what I did. Dumbass." And if Agnes had to catch the orb, she probably would have insisted on holding onto it while I climbed the ladder, and I wouldn't have argued with her.

Back on the streets of Sumer II, the entire city seemed alive, and in this city, I wouldn't have been surprised if the buildings really did sprout legs and run after us, kinda like that Russian witch's hut on chicken legs, which reminded me... "Hey, Agnes, is Baba Yaga like your cousin or something? Or just an alternate personality?"

Agnes held out an orb and said, "Don't make me use this on you."

"How do you know who Baba Yaga is, anyway?" Frey asked.

So I shrugged and reminded him there was a dead god living inside my head who'd obviously known all kinds of useless shit.

"The wall is this way," Enki said, pointing toward the interior of the city.

"Um, we just came from that direction," Joachim said.

We shot each other suspicious glances, and I really began to regret ever trusting these Sumerian gods. Enki shook his head and insisted, "It's part of Asalluhi's illusion and why it took you so long to find Frey. If you head in the direction where you think the wall is, you'll find yourself back in a maze of deadly alleys with monsters lurking at every corner. I know these buildings, and where they are in relation to each other and the city's wall."

We must've still looked entirely too suspicious because Ninhursag added, "If you don't want our help, we'll part ways here. But your friend doesn't have a lot of time, so whatever you choose, make your decision quickly."

It seemed really unfair to play on our fears about Tyr like that, but at the same time, she was right. He was running out of time.

"Okay," I said. "Lead the way, but don't let my village idiot demeanor fool you. I'm a lot deadlier than I look."

Agnes snorted and asked when "deadlier" had become synonymous with "dumber" so I snatched my orb from her hand and threatened to throw it at her.

Wait. What I meant was, if she actually *had* my orb, I would've snatched it from her hand and threatened to throw it at her.

Enki rolled his eyes, and sure, I probably deserved it, but since I still suspected he was leading us into a trap, I totally resented it, so I mumbled, "*You're* the village idiot" at his back as he walked toward the city's center. Of course, I should've waited until his wife moved away from me to declare Enki was Sumer II's resident idiot, but she just rolled her eyes at me, too, and followed her husband.

Agnes shook her head at me and said, "Don't worry, Gavyn. You're in no danger of losing your crown anytime soon."

"Shouldn't you be chasing down your hut?" I snapped.

"Baba Yaga's hut only *turns* on its legs, dumbass," she snapped back.

I nodded seriously. "You would know."

We'd made it a block before any of us had to use one of Ninhursag's paralyzing orbs. And when we did, it was on what appeared to be a herd of half-serpent, half-leopard monsters. Thor was the first to throw his orb, so we held onto ours as we waited to see if Ninhursag's magic would work on hideous freaks of nature. I mean, she hadn't used them on the Hellhounds…

"Hey, Ninny!" I demanded. "Why didn't you use these against those devil dogs?"

"First of all, don't call me that. And secondly, if I'd used one in such a confined space, I'd have risked paralyzing all of us, too, so we'd be helpless but totally conscious as any dogs that hadn't been paralyzed ate us alive," she said.

I blinked at her then turned my attention back to the serpopards. "Never mind."

On the opposite street, a demigod gang ran toward us, so I hurled my orb at their feet. Like the monsters on our other side, they froze as soon as that magical blue mist escaped its glass prison. But our enemies knew where we were now, and we only had three orbs left.

"Run!" Enki shouted. I looked over my shoulder and saw why. Someone had retrieved the surviving Hellhounds, and those bastards were *still* whispering my name.

"That's it," I yelled as I ran. "I need to learn their names, too, then I'm going to whisper them as I chop their damn heads off!" But even with our supernatural genes, those devil dogs were faster, forcing Agnes to throw her orb.

And now, we were down to two with at least a block to go.

"*Don't think, don't think, don't think,*" I reminded myself. And you wouldn't expect that to be difficult for me, but apparently, the one time I needed to truly embrace my role as the world's foremost, preeminent idiot was the one time my brain refused to cooperate. As we ran, I realized, much to my horror, that I'd been *thinking*.

"Aw, damn it," I groaned aloud.

Agnes shot me a curious look, but the explosion in front of us answered her unspoken question of "What now?"

I held my shield over our heads as debris rained on us and she put a hand on her hip and said, "What did you do?"

"I may have thought we had to be almost to the wall by now, and we should be able to get out of Sumer II after all."

"Tyr?" Thor said. "Tyr?" His voice had taken on an urgent tone, and Agnes darted out from beneath the safety of my shield to hurry to Tyr's side. The war god had slumped over, and no amount of shaking and calling his name could rouse him.

"You have to get us out of here now!" I shouted at Enki. Thor handed Frey his hammer then lifted Tyr and slung him over his shoulder like a sack of flour, and I gaped stupidly for a few seconds at just how *massively* strong the guy was before urging Enki and Ninhursag to hurry. They took off running again, and we followed, leaping over piles of rubble from the explosion. As we turned a corner, which looked like it would bring us farther into the heart of this labyrinth, I saw the wall stretching before us instead. But the Sumerians had no intention of letting us out of here that easily, and a line of gods and heroes stood ready to bar our exit.

Ninhursag clutched one orb and Joachim had the other, but the line of Sumerian warriors was spread out, meaning it was unlikely we'd be able to paralyze them all. Ninhursag slowed and whispered to Joachim, "Wait until we're almost close enough to engage in sword fights then choose the densest pack on your right. I'll monitor the left."

Joachim nodded in acknowledgment, and we all slowed as the gods and demigods gradually began to move closer to one another in anticipation of fighting us before we could reach the hole in the wall. They obviously knew by now that Ninhursag had helped us escape with one of her magical orbs, though, and they were careful not to stand too close to each other.

"We've been through far too much Hell to die this close to freedom," I said quietly. "Get through the wall and get Tyr to a hospital. I'll distract them."

Of all the gods I expected an argument from, Agnes was the last one I'd have thought would speak first or so vehemently. She grabbed my arm and forced me to look at her. "We're *all* getting out of here. Now stop acting like such a—"

"A hero?" Thor finished for her.

Agnes narrowed her eyes at the god of thunder, but Ninhursag whispered, "On the count of three, everyone run. We'll paralyze as many as possible and fight the rest."

"This is a terrible idea," I complained, but everyone ignored me.

"One," Ninhursag said.

I tried estimating how many gods and demigods waited for us at the wall, but my brain had finally decided to listen to me and refused to function.

"Two."

This was it: Custer's Last Stand, and my malfunctioning brain seemed to vaguely remember it hadn't ended so well for that guy.

"Three!"

But despite my many reservations, I wouldn't let my friends go without me, so I did the only thing I could.

I ran.

CHAPTER FOUR

I'll be honest: I'm not really sure *how* we got through that wall. I remember swarms of gods and demigods descending on us, and Ninhursag and Joachim throwing their orbs, but ultimately, we'd had to fight our way out. At least, I *think* we had to fight our way out. In the end, none of us could actually remember it that well, and we all had conflicting accounts of how we actually escaped. Perhaps it'd been one last trick by the Sumerian god of magic, or maybe extremely stressful situations just had that effect on people, but whatever the reason, by the time we stopped running in that wheat field outside of Sumer II's wall so we could cross the veil, none of us were quite sure how we'd gotten there.

Enki and Ninhursag crossed with us, because they couldn't stay behind now that everyone knew they'd helped us escape. So we found ourselves back at the hotel in Baton Rouge with two extra gods who just happened to be the mother and stepfather of my greatest, mortal enemy, and a Norse god on the brink of death. And actually, as Thor lowered him carefully to the floor to check on him, we realized Tyr wasn't breathing.

"Oh, my God," Agnes gasped. She dropped to the floor beside him and began CPR, so naturally, my mouth fell open and my brain decided it would be a good use of my time to ask a hundred ridiculous questions. Who was going around teaching *gods* CPR? And when gods said, "Oh, my God," who were they talking to? *The* god? Their best friend? Themselves?

Only Joachim was really paying attention to me though, and he just nodded and said, "All good questions."

A door opened down the hallway, and Keira rushed out of her room, running then throwing herself at me, wrapping me in her arms and holding me so tightly, I thought *this* was what Heaven must be like. But she'd clearly been convinced we were all dead, and Tyr kinda *was*, so I just told her, "Hey, I'm all right. And an ambulance is on the way for Tyr."

"But you were gone for three days!" she cried.

"What?" I breathed.

Three days? How was that even possible? I was absolutely certain none of us had slept or ate while we were in Sumer, so it couldn't *possibly* have been that long. But my stomach burned and gurgled, and I realized I actually was starving, and with the adrenaline of our escape wearing off, I wasn't just exhausted... I could hardly keep myself from falling over.

Each one of us that had just come from Sumer II, except for Enki and Ninhursag who waited a respectful distance from our reunited group, seemed to become aware of just how tired and hungry we really were, but we also refused to leave Tyr's side until the paramedics arrived. Apparently, Agnes had managed to get him breathing again, but his breaths were shallow and his skin remained cool and clammy.

I felt sick watching them load my friend onto a gurney, wheeling him out of the hotel. Ull and Odin went with them, and as the elevator doors closed and I could no longer see him, I finally let Keira drag me into my room where she told me to lie down while she ordered room service. She was so breathtakingly beautiful. "You thought I was dead."

Keira placed the handset back on the cradle and nodded, but she wouldn't look at me.

"Even though you've already been told how I'm going to die, and I'm pretty sure it wasn't in Sumer II."

She just nodded again, but this time, she took a deep breath and said, "Tyr is supposed to die at Ragnarok, but that doesn't mean he'll pull through now."

"So prophecies *can* change," I argued.

"Dead is dead, Gavyn. I don't think it matters so much *how* a person dies."

I thought it did, especially since Tyr's death was presumably thousands of years away. And if I were destined to live that long, I'd be kinda pissed about being cheated out of millennia of life. But since I was human, or at least part human, I'd never expected to live that long anyway, and I'd kinda accepted my fate. But I hadn't accepted Keira's refusal to admit she was falling for me, too, and her concern for me, her refusal to leave my side now... *that's* what I cared about far more than proving I was right about these prophecies.

"But you thought I was dead, and that upset you... and not just because you think you need me to defeat the Sumerians," I pressed.

"Gavyn," she sighed, but at least she looked at me now.

"Keira," I sighed back. "You can't pretend like I'm just another hero to you."

I thought she was going to tell me that was exactly what I was, or that it was complicated, or that it was her job to protect me. But her eyebrows pulled together and she said, "I've never pretended you were just another hero to me. And you already know you're not."

"But..." There was always a "but," and I knew it was coming. Hell, you know it's coming, too, right?

"But," she continued, "if there's even a chance I can save you, I'm going to take it."

I wanted to ask her what she meant, what our relationship had to do with my death or her ability to save me, but I fell asleep. I mean, seriously. I was just lying there, fighting off the sheer exhaustion of three days with no sleep and battling monsters and demigods and an insane labyrinth, talking to the woman who could quite possibly be the love of my short, pathetic life, and I *fell asleep*.

Loser.

I awoke seventeen hours later, my stomach still empty and burning, but I was alone in my room, which only reminded me Yngvarr was supposed to be with me. I found the container of food Keira had left me in the mini-fridge then stumbled into the hallway, shoving fistfuls of fries into my mouth between yawns. With my hands full, I couldn't knock on her door, so I kicked it instead and kept kicking it until Agnes yanked it open, looking even older and more wrinkled than ever.

"Baba Yaga," I said, nodding as if I were actually greeting Baba Yaga.

"What do you want, Gavyn?" she sighed.

"I'm assuming you checked on Yngvarr already, so I was—"

"Um, I'm fine," Yngvarr said from *inside her room*.

My nose instinctively wrinkled in disgust and I yelled back, "Dude!"

"Oh, relax," Agnes said. "His leg is all stitched up and he's still recuperating. It's not like anything *could* happen."

"No, nothing could happen because you're like a million years old," I retorted. But I walked past her anyway to scowl at Yngvarr, who owed me an industrial sized can of brain bleach.

I set my cold burger and fries on the table and pretended

to be interested in the newspaper for a few moments, unable to ask about Tyr but needing to know at the same time. Agnes finally sat on her bed and said my name far too quietly, far too kindly.

So I shook my head and responded with the only word I *could*. "Ragnarok."

Agnes and Yngvarr exchanged a confused glance, and she tried again. "Gavyn, he's on life support. We all have to be prepared for the fact that he may not make it home."

"A god is on life support," I said flatly.

Yngvarr shrugged. "We don't have better technology in Asgard."

"Don't you have some medicine god who can heal him?" I cried, but really, I was begging.

"No," Yngvarr answered, his voice sad and resigned. "We have gods who can heal minor things, but not something like this. We're not omnipotent."

"Odin is staying with Tyr," Agnes said, "so I've got someone coming to help us."

I sank into a chair at the table and rubbed my eyes with the heel of my hands. "Help with what? What did we miss over the past three days?"

"Where do you want me to start?" Yngvarr asked.

I grunted at him, so he just held up a hand and started ticking off fingers. "Medeina has shown up in Moscow and taken over the government. Again. And—"

"As a wolf or a woman?" I interrupted.

"Does it matter?" Agnes asked.

I shrugged. "I'd kinda like to see how a wolf takes over an entire country."

Yngvarr blinked at me so I flicked my wrist at him as if I were giving him permission to speak. "You may continue."

He ticked off another finger but eyed me suspiciously like he just knew I'd never be able to keep my mouth shut.

"Paricia has been causing so many tidal waves, the government of Peru surrendered to spare lives."

"But no more demons, right?"

"No," he assured me. "They were apparently uniquely attached to Supay, who's dead now, so we're not entirely sure where those demons are or who's controlling them."

"Inti and Mama Pacha have been trying to get Paricia under control," Agnes added. "But so far, Paricia seems to be winning the battle for their heroes' allegiance."

"And then there's the surviving Egyptian gods," Yngvarr said. "The CIA thinks they're in the U.S. still and may have some sort of agreement with the Sumerians, perhaps something like taking over America first then the world. After they've achieved that, the Sumerians will hand Egypt over to their allies."

"And now for the good news," I pleaded

"Well, like I said," Agnes offered. "I've got a friend who'll be joining us soon."

"A friend. As in singular... one."

She crossed her arms defiantly and snapped, "We're Tuatha Dé. We don't need superior numbers."

"Besides," Yngvarr said. "I've heard great things about Nuada and—"

"Whoa," I interrupted again, "the guy with the silver arm?"

"Gavyn," he groaned, but I hadn't been finished when he interrupted *me*, so I had to interrupt back.

"What's the deal? One god with a prosthetic hand is hospitalized, so we have to replace him with another maimed god?"

"Gavyn, he—" Agnes started, but I *still* wasn't finished.

"And how does it even work? Is it like Bucky's?"

Agnes's look of total annoyance shifted to utter confusion. "Bucky? Who the hell is Bucky?"

"Bucky Barnes," I said as if that explained everything. Agnes just kept staring at me, so I threw my hands up in a gesture of very real disbelief and my own annoyance. "Y'all made me read your ridiculous myths, but you don't know who Bucky Barnes is? That's it. Marvel movie marathon, right now."

Agnes's nine-thousand-year-old mouth fell open before she grabbed one of her pillows and threw it at me. "I can't believe you're wasting my time over a fictional character!"

A knock on her door saved me from having more pillows thrown at my head, and Agnes shuffled to the door, muttering to herself about fate's twisted sense of humor for making *me* any kind of hero, which I actually completely agreed with. As soon as she opened the door, I saw Keira standing in the hallway, but she wasn't alone. From my angle, though, I couldn't see who she was with. "Is Gavyn in here?" Keira asked. "I can't find him."

Agnes grunted and waved them inside, and I immediately decided I didn't like these newcomers, especially one of them. I mean, I'm totally straight, but even I could tell that guy was a good-looking dude, and I may have been a little threatened by him.

"What are you doing in here?" Keira asked me.

"Babysitting," I answered. "What are *you* doing here?"

"Looking for you, so I can introduce you to our allies. Gavyn, this is Anubis." I stood up and shook the guy's hand, because he wasn't the one I'd already decided I hated.

"So what exactly does a god of the dead *do*?" I asked him.

"Somebody warned you about Gavyn, right?" Agnes asked him.

Both Anubis and Most Loathsome God in the Universe nodded.

"And this is Ra," Keira said.

Ra held out his hand, and I narrowed my eyes at it like he

was trying to hand me an asp, but not just any asp... the one that killed Cleopatra. I wasn't really sure *why* it had to be the same venomous snake that killed Cleopatra, but it was. The sun god glanced at his hand then at me and let his hand fall.

Keira shot me a look that warned me to stop embarrassing her, so I forced a smile in Ra's direction and said, "Sorry. You just reminded me of someone I knew a long time ago."

And Agnes, being the witchy pain in the ass she was, just *had* to pipe in. "Oh, yeah? Who?"

So I narrowed my eyes at *her* and snapped, "Don't you have children to drown, Jenny Greenteeth?"

And *why* had Havard known so much useless trivia?

"She supposedly drowned adults, too, so if I'm impersonating her, guess who I'll start with?" Agnes said.

"Yngvarr, but since he used to be your lover, I think he's been through enough psychological trauma," I responded.

Agnes rolled her eyes then decided to ignore me. "Ra, please forgive our village idiot. We're all convinced he really can't help it."

But Ra was stealing glances at Yngvarr with a look on his face that we could all easily interpret... it was something along the lines of, "Why the bloody hell were you in a relationship with *her*?" and quite likely "Dude... ew," and "I need hospital-grade brain bleach. Stat."

So Yngvarr sighed and said, "She doesn't always look like this. Because of a curse on everyone who knew Gavyn's ancestor, I can't remember ever being in a relationship with her, but I'm positive it was always her young, hot self."

"I wasn't judging," Ra lied.

But now Agnes was feeling defensive, so she crossed her arms again and scowled at Yngvarr. "So what... you were only dating me for my body? You wouldn't have loved me for *me* if I looked like this?"

"Um," Yngvarr stammered, "Badb, I—"

"Agnes," I corrected.

Everyone was apparently still ignoring me.

"I don't remember how I felt," he tried, but Agnes still looked pissed and hurt, which was totally unfair, of course, but since I didn't want to be turned into a frog, I decided to stay out of it.

Fortunately, Keira had grown tired of listening to our ridiculous conversation and scolded us all. "Tyr is literally fighting for his life right now, we have gods all over the world hurting innocent people, and Ra and Anubis didn't come here to listen to immature, pointless arguments."

"Sorry," we all mumbled.

Ra kept shooting me weird looks, like he was trying to figure out what the hell my problem was, and I kinda wanted to save him the time by telling him no one knew, least of all me, but since I hated the guy for being an Egyptian Adonis who was standing way too closely to Keira, I just shot him weird looks, too.

"Gavyn," Keira said, "whatever you're doing, stop."

"I'm not doing anything," I lied, and for good measure, added, "Besides, he started it."

"Oh, my God," Keira said. "What are you... six?"

"Eight," I immediately replied then flashed her a mischievous grin. "Oh, you meant my *age*."

"Oh, my God," Keira repeated.

"I'm going to see what's taking Nuada so long," Agnes interjected, but she gave me the side-eye that screamed, "I'm really just trying to get away from you," and there was quite likely a "dumbass" in there, too.

Keira turned to Yngvarr and asked, "Can you fill Ra and Anubis in on what's going on here with the CIA? I need to talk to Gavyn alone."

Crap.

Okay, so maybe I shouldn't have embarrassed her like that, but in my defense, Ra really did start it by existing.

I sheepishly followed Keira to her room, phrasing different apologies in my head depending on what specifically I had to apologize for. But as soon as she closed her door, she said, "I talked to Odin about the sword in his palace."

"Oh," I breathed. My sword. The Sword of Secrets and Light and Prophecy. How had I forgotten the importance of its discovery?

"He claims he doesn't remember who made it, or how he even got it," she continued. "When I told him about your dream and Havard giving that exact sword to Arnbjorg as a wedding present, he said he must've bought it from one of their descendants."

I scoffed because that just seemed like something I should scoff at.

Keira nodded like she was internally scoffing with me. "If there's one thing I know about my father, it's that he doesn't forget so easily. It's possible that this sword is somehow connected to Havard's curse though, so maybe he really doesn't remember."

I sat on the edge of my bed and put my head in my hands. I'd just slept seventeen hours. How could I still be so tired? "We *have* to find my sword, Keira."

"I know," she assured me. "And we will. I really believe these memories are clues, and we just have to put this puzzle together."

"Yeah," I sighed. "But I can't help feeling like we're running out of time, like the Sumerians are only a minor problem and the bigger threat is right in front of us."

Keira sat beside me and took a deep breath. "Inanna knew about Havard *and* his sword. She lied about it being Sumerian, but how did she even know about it? And why do the Sumerians want it so badly?"

"To keep it out of my hands," I answered. "They know if I find it, they'll lose."

"I guess the real question, then, is who among our family *wants* us to lose?"

"We have a traitor," I agreed.

When Keira met my gaze, my chest began to ache from the sorrow in her eyes. Part of me wished I'd kept my mouth shut, even though I almost always failed at that, and part of me wished she'd just let me hold her. But she surprised the hell out of me when she rested her head on my shoulder and didn't pull away when I put my arms around her. "Yes, Gavyn," she whispered. "We have a traitor."

ARNBJORG ROCKS HAVARD'S WORLD

(Not like that—get your minds out of the gutter)

Almost two months had passed since the happiest day of my life, the day Arnbjorg married me and our journey toward forever began. Finn had put on weight and was adjusting well to life in Asgard and had even attracted the attention of a young goddess, a daughter of Forseti whom everyone admired.

My life was almost perfect. And on that day almost two months from the date of our wedding, Arnbjorg found me in the stables and completed that circle of perfection. "You lavish as much attention on Sigurd as you do me," she teased.

I glanced over my shoulder at her and smiled. "You will always be first, my love."

Arnbjorg rubbed Sigurd's neck, and he whinnied softly. I often thought he cared for her more than me, and I couldn't blame him at all. "Yngvarr is beside himself. He can't sit still," she said.

"I know. That's why I'm out here. He was driving me crazy."

My wife flashed me a sly smile and said, "He's in love,

Havard. And this will be the first time Badb has come to Asgard. He wants to impress her."

I tossed aside the brush I'd been using on Sigurd's coat and told her, "You'll like her. She's fierce and powerful and although she's beautiful, she never relies on her looks to accomplish anything, even if most men would readily capitulate. But she knows she doesn't have to—she's strong and lets others know to treat her as the powerful goddess she is."

"I *do* like her already," Arnbjorg agreed.

I hadn't seen Badb since our hunting trip to Ljósálfheim. I'd only left Asgard once since my wedding, and that was to retrieve Finn. But Yngvarr spoke of Badb so often, I felt as if the war goddess and I were old friends, and I was admittedly looking forward to her visit.

Arnbjorg was still combing her fingers along Sigurd's smooth coat when she asked, "What do you want more than anything, Havard?"

"You," I immediately answered.

She smiled but shook her head. "You already have me. For eternity, and if there were anything beyond, you'd have me then, too. I meant something you don't have."

I already knew my answer, but I took my time responding, parsing out words to ensure I didn't upset her. Because what I wanted most now was the same thing her heart longed for. Truthfully, I was also afraid of hoping too soon.

"I would gladly welcome children," I finally said. "But you should never feel as if you aren't enough for me to be far happier than I have any right to be."

Arnbjorg stopped petting Sigurd, and her smile pulled higher. "In that case, how much happier will you be when our child is born?"

"Arnbjorg," I breathed. "Do you mean—"

"Yes," she laughed.

I threw my arms around her and lifted her from the

ground, twirling her briefly before realizing pregnancy often made women sick and I likely wasn't helping. But we were only months away from that perfect life, and while I didn't know how long we'd be able to enjoy it together, I was absolutely certain it would be worth it. I would die still believing I was the luckiest god in Asgard.

Outside, we heard Yngvarr calling for us and correctly assumed Badb had arrived. With her striking red hair, I immediately recognized the war goddess and began to approach her, but Arnbjorg tugged on my hand to slow me down and whispered, "Let's not tell them yet. Yngvarr has been so excited. Let him enjoy having Badb here for a while before everyone's attention shifts to us."

I kissed her forehead and agreed; that was my Arnbjorg, always so thoughtful and selfless.

But that night, I couldn't sleep, so I snuck outside to watch Nótt track across the sky. I couldn't have been sitting there more than a few minutes when I heard footsteps in the grass and turned to see Badb coming toward me.

"Couldn't sleep?" I asked. "Will Yngvarr not leave you alone?"

She laughed and sat beside me, tipping her face toward the night sky and Nótt's faintly illuminated chariot. "You've got it backwards, Havard. Yngvarr is worn out and fast asleep. I couldn't wake him if I tried."

"You must not have tried then."

She arched an eyebrow at me and replied, "Why do you think I'm out here with you rather than in his room?"

It was my turn to laugh. "And what do you think of Asgard?" I asked.

She shot me a mischievous grin and said, "It's almost as lovely as the Otherworld."

"You aren't going to steal my brother, are you?"

"I'd never ask him to leave his family just as he'd never ask me to leave mine. Odin has extended an open invitation to me so that I may return to Asgard as often as I like just as King Nuada has done for Yngvarr."

"Nuada's going to regret that," I teased.

Badb smiled and lifted a shoulder. "I sincerely doubt it."

"You'll keep going back and forth then?" I pressed. "Do you think it will work?" It hadn't worked for Njord and Skadi, and I feared my brother's heart was in danger.

"For now," she answered carefully. "Whatever's in our future, we'll handle together."

"The future," I sighed. I wondered what it must be like to have a completely uncertain fate, to be able to live each day with such mystery and possibility.

Badb touched my shoulder and gave me a look of concern and compassion, so I resolved to trust this goddess as much as my brother did. "Can you keep a secret?" I asked her.

"Oh," she whispered. But she nodded and waited, so I told her I'd been having dreams that were really prophecies and would one day need her help.

"My help?" she repeated. "What are these prophecies and why would you need my help and not Yngvarr's?"

I could tell by the tone of her voice she was worried these prophecies would be dangerous for my brother, which only reinforced in my mind that I'd made the right decision in placing my faith in this goddess. She would defend my brother regardless of personal costs. "I can't talk to Yngvarr about this," I replied. "Every time I try, he refuses to listen or accept I can do nothing to prevent my fate. But I know I'm going to die, and I think it'll be to protect my children. How could I possibly accept an alternative future when my children's lives are at stake?"

"Your children," she said. "So this isn't a prophecy that will come to fruition anytime soon."

"I'm not sure," I admitted. "But I can't trust anyone

among the Aesir. I don't recognize the god who kills me with my sword, but it happens here in Asgard, which means someone let him in."

"And you need something from me," Badb guessed. "Do you need me to ensure Arnbjorg is cared for?"

I swallowed and checked on Nótt's progress across Asgard's dark sky. It was painful to say this part aloud. "No," I said quietly. "I don't think she'll survive either. We both sacrifice ourselves for our children."

"Havard," she started, but she fumbled with words before finding the ones she wanted. "We need to figure out who is responsible for this and how your surrender protects your children. We'll—"

"Badb," I interrupted, "this is exactly how Yngvarr reacts when I try to talk to him about this prophecy. You know well that we can't escape our fates though. When Arnbjorg and I agree to hand over my sword and surrender to this mystery god, it's because *he's* agreed to allow our children to escape to Midgard and live. And truly, Arnbjorg and I don't want to be separated, neither in life nor in death."

Badb sighed and offered me a sad, sympathetic glance. "You're lucky to love someone so much."

"Do you?" I asked. I'd seen the way she and Yngvarr looked at one another, and I already knew the answer. But I wanted to hear it from her, to know that when Arnbjorg and I were gone, he wouldn't be alone. Our sisters would still be here, of course, but they were so busy with their own families, and it wouldn't be the same anyway. Yngvarr would need the comfort of the goddess he loved as much as I loved my wife.

"Yes," she whispered.

"Yngvarr will one day lose not only his brother but his best friend. He'll need you."

"I'll be here," Badb promised.

"My sword... it's no ordinary sword. The enchantment

only works for me, but if a magician is powerful enough, he may be able to figure out how to cast a new enchantment on it. I'll have to hand it over to this god one day. I need you to retrieve it."

Badb made a strange croaking noise, and her eyes widened but she took a deep breath and seemed to think about my request before saying, "All right. I'll do my best. What should I do with it if I'm successful? Bring it to Yngvarr?"

"No, you need to hide it. We can't risk it falling into the wrong hands. This sword is far too powerful. And there will be someone who needs it one day."

"But everyone will know about it," she argued. "They'll keep looking for this sword, and I doubt there's any place in any world where I could guarantee its safety."

"Yes," I agreed. "If people remember it, they'll continue to hunt for it, which is why we'll ensure no one knows about the Sword of Prophecy until it's time for my descendant to claim it and all its power."

Badb bit her lip and considered this then nodded. "I'll help you, Havard. When the time comes, I'll avenge your murder and retrieve your sword. And you will ensure no one, not even me, remembers the Sword of Prophecy."

For the first time since the dreams of my fate began, the burden of this knowledge lightened, and I felt oddly calm and at peace. "Thank you, Badb. I hope fate will reward you for this."

Badb turned back to Nótt's chariot and took one last deep breath. "I love your brother, Havard. More than I've ever loved anyone. If some god is conspiring against your family, I'll gladly risk my life to protect his."

"Then that's what we'll do, Badb. We'll protect him and both of our families. No matter what."

Badb smiled faintly and put a hand over mine. "Yes," she said. "No matter what."

CHAPTER SIX

Agnes sat across from me, sipping on her coffee and occasionally tapping her eight-thousand-year-old fingers against her paper cup. When I finished recounting this latest dream, I asked her if *any* of it rang a bell, but she lifted a wrinkled, spotted hand and cut me off. "Do you really think if I had any memories of this, I wouldn't have shared them?"

"How should I know? Maybe it's part of your coven's secret agreement," I shot back.

Agnes squinted at me and asked, "What kind of secret agreements do covens have?"

"Again: how should I know? *I'm* not a witch."

Agnes fell silent for a few moments, obviously deep in thought, so I assumed she was concentrating on the ancient terms of her covenant. Or she was trying to recall the spell to turn me into a frog, which honestly wouldn't have been *that* bad. It would've gotten me out of having to fight more shapeshifting gods or flaming zombie monkeys.

"What do you think went wrong?" she finally asked.

My brain was still fixated on flaming zombie monkeys, so

I blinked at her and answered, "Um... I'm thinking they took a wrong turn when they lit him on fire, because really, the flames just made him easier to track."

Not surprisingly, Agnes blinked back at me and sighed loudly. "Gavyn... *what?*"

"Maybe you should provide a little more context," I suggested, trying to sound like it was really her fault I had no idea what she was talking about and not mine for being completely unable to follow a simple conversation.

"This spell," Agnes explained slowly. "It sounds like Havard and I had something to do with his curse. But why would I have agreed to it if it meant I'd have to forget Yngvarr?"

"To protect him?" I guessed. "It seemed like Havard was just planning on some spell to make people forget the sword, not necessarily him and Arnbjorg. So maybe something went wrong. We still don't know who murdered Havard or why, but Yngvarr may have been in danger. And based on the way you were talking about him, you would've done anything to keep him safe."

Even as I said it, I cringed internally, mostly because I was sitting across from Eve herself.

"Yeah," she said absentmindedly. "I think I would have." She caught me giving her a look of utter disgust, so she cleared her throat and sat up straighter. "Have you told anyone else about this dream?"

"No, not even Keira."

"Good," she said. "Until we know more, it's best not to make everyone suspicious of everyone else."

"Honestly, my list of suspects is pretty short."

Agnes shrugged. "We have no idea yet if it was a single traitor or an elaborate conspiracy. If you have to talk to someone else, confide in Yngvarr but that's it."

"What about Keira?"

"Keira's father is on your list, and you said she adopted a son who must tie in somehow. And you don't know yet what that boy will look like when he gets older."

I opened my mouth to tell her Áki couldn't possibly be Havard's murderer, but he *did* have a motive. After all, Havard had been one of the gods responsible for his family's slaughter, and he'd ordered Áki's death, too.

Yeah, I'd say that was plenty of motive.

"Okay," I agreed. "Only trust Yngvarr with this information."

"One more thing. If I'm the one who avenged Havard's murder, I must've hidden the sword, right?"

"Yeah, that's what Havard asked you to do. Do you think it's in the Otherworld?"

Agnes shook her head. "No, I think it's in Asgard. I'd want to make sure the descendant who was supposed to inherit it could find it."

I grunted at her and sank back in my chair. "Then maybe I'm not the heir, and that's why I can't find it."

"Gavyn, these dreams are part of the curse. They're intended to lead you to the Sword of Light when you're ready to wield its power."

"I'm ready!" I exclaimed, but really, I just wanted a weapon that could easily kill Ninurta. Of course, since I was fated to die, I suspected I'd never find Havard's sword, because if I had it, how could Ninurta or anyone else kill me?

Yngvarr knocked on Agnes's door and called out to her, asking if I were with her and letting us know Nuada had arrived. Admittedly, I kinda wanted to meet this king of the Tuatha Dé to see if he had a silver arm like the Winter Soldier, and if I could get one the next time a supernatural wolf tried to rip my arm off.

But with Yngvarr at the door, Agnes immediately transformed into the redheaded beauty, so I narrowed my eyes at her to indicate I really didn't appreciate having to converse with the Wicked Witch of the West while Yngvarr got to hang out with Glinda. But she ignored me anyway, so my silent protest was pretty useless as all of my protests were.

As Nuada followed Yngvarr into the room, I studied his disappointingly normal arms, and of course Agnes saw me and mumbled, "Dumbass."

"Which arm is the fake one?" I asked Nuada. "You obviously have way better orthotists than the Norse."

"Why do you even know what an orthotist is?" Yngvarr asked.

I had no idea, actually. "I know things," I snapped.

Nuada glanced between me and Agnes then asked her, "What's his problem?"

"Your guess is as good as ours," she answered.

I crossed my arms and pouted. "I thought you'd have a silver arm."

"Who do you think I am? Bucky Barnes?"

I turned to Agnes and said, "I like him. Let's keep him."

Agnes rolled her eyes, but before she could chastise me for being a childish idiot, Yngvarr said, "We have a strange problem."

"Great," I groaned. "Let me guess: shapeshifting asshole gods. We *finally* have to confront a poisonous deer."

"Um... no."

"Demons? Wait... devil dogs. I swear to God, if it's devil dogs, I'm outta here."

"Please tell us before he keeps talking," Agnes begged.

Yngvarr nodded and said, "It's the Mississippi River."

"The river?" I repeated. "Is it flooding?" We had spillways now to prevent major cities from flooding, but with gods who could control the environment, I wouldn't have been surprised if the city flooded anyway.

But Yngvarr shook his head. "I think you need to see this for yourself," he said carefully.

Agnes and I exchanged a nervous glance, and I even lost interest in trying to figure out if Nuada really had a fake arm. "Yngvarr, what's going on?"

He took a deep breath and ran his fingers through his hair. "We don't actually know. But it *looks* like the river has turned into blood."

"This is so gross," I complained as I stared down at the river from the top of the levee. Traffic had been halted, both on the river and over the bridges, and the barges that had been en route to New Orleans were anchored by the banks. Thick, dark waves stained the sides of ships and the riverboat where I'd once lost three hundred dollars playing Texas hold 'em, a game I apparently hadn't really understood. In my defense, I'd been a little drunk, which was pretty much how most of my stories that involved losing significant amounts of money started.

"The Department of Environmental Quality just announced it *is* blood," Agnes said, obviously reading the news on her smartphone. "And it's human."

"What the hell?" I murmured. "I'm assuming millions of people weren't slaughtered upriver or anything."

Agnes shook her head. "No reports of large numbers of missing people or bodies floating in the river. And it's not river water mixed with blood... we're looking at an actual river of blood."

"Ew," I complained. "And why are we still here looking at this?"

"There's really nothing we can do," Nuada agreed. "They're evacuating homes and businesses all along the river.

I doubt it poses an immediate threat to any humans, but since no one knows why the river has turned into blood, they just want to be on the safe side. Somebody will take responsibility for this soon, and we'll respond accordingly."

"Yeah," I said. "And when—" A large green striped frog jumped on my shoe, so I kicked it off and tried again. "I'm willing to bet the Sumerians—"

A croaking sound interrupted me yet again, so I sighed impatiently and glanced at the ground by my feet where another large, striped frog was apparently trying to get my attention. "Agnes," I said, "did you turn your former lovers into frogs?"

"Don't be ridiculous," she replied. "If I could turn people into frogs, *you'd* be the one croaking on the ground right now."

I nodded in agreement. "Sounds about right." To the frog, I added, "Don't make me kick you into the bloody river. Get out of here."

His throat expanded and he croaked at me again, so I decided my time probably wasn't being well spent arguing with an amphibian. "As I was saying, the Sumerians—"

Several frogs croaked simultaneously, and we each turned around, peering down at the street on the opposite side of the levee. "Holy shit," I mumbled.

"This is so much worse than the river," Yngvarr added.

We *all* nodded, because the street below us had filled with jumping green bodies, and inexplicably, more frogs seemed to be coming out of every doorway and window of every building along the street. Bullfrogs spilled from parked cars, and when I glanced down river toward the *U.S.S. Kidd*, the old destroyer was equally covered. Its deck had come alive with the oddly pulsing movement of thousands of frogs leaping over one another, but the frogs kept tumbling from *somewhere* as if the ship itself were bleeding amphibians.

The entire city seemed to come alive, and the Mississippi River Bridge rained bullfrogs into the river below. Even though my eyes kept telling my brain Baton Rouge was being overrun with frogs and our rivers had turned to blood, my brain refused to believe it. I was convinced this all had to be an illusion, even as huge frogs beat against my legs and piled so thickly around our feet, we'd crush them if we tried to move. And not only was I typically against killing animals for no reason, I *really* didn't want to get frog guts all over my shoes.

"Oh, God," I groaned as I glanced between the frogs surrounding us and the crimson river.

"What?" Agnes asked. She'd moved closer to Yngvarr and was watching the frogs with so much disgust, I half expected her to invoke some kind of curse on the city and burn the whole place to the ground.

"River of blood," I said, batting down one particularly obnoxious frog that tried to leap at my face. "Frogs overrunning the city. What does this sound like?"

My allies stared at me for a few seconds as if not believing this could actually be happening to a city in the twenty-first century. "The Ten Plagues of Egypt," Yngvarr gasped, also swatting away frogs that were piling thicker and thicker around us. They were up to our knees now.

"Yeah," I said, cringing as I pulled a bullfrog off my shoulder. "Which means this is only the beginning. Baton Rouge is about to become Hell on Earth."

CHAPTER SEVEN

Over half a million people had to be evacuated from their homes and relocated because of frogs. *Frogs.* Sure, we all suspected worse things were coming, but the Mississippi River transforming into blood just freaked people out. Few people who didn't live near the river left the city when the Mississippi turned into blood. It was the frogs that made government officials issue a mandatory evacuation order. Every surface of the city, every road and building and bridge, was covered with frogs, so when the hundreds of thousands of cars from the metropolitan area took to the streets... well, I'm sure you can imagine how that played out. At least it was late fall, and the cooler temperatures meant all those squished frog bodies weren't baking in near hundred-degree temperatures, but still.

Even as I stood in my hotel room, I watched the damn things tumbling from the roof. Cars were essentially parked on the interstate in the distance, the heavy traffic paralyzing an entire city. Most of the vehicles had been covered in green and brown amphibians like they were some kind of swamp monster from a cheesy '50s horror flick. Keira joined me by the window and shuddered. "How will they ever get rid of millions of bullfrogs?"

"If they release millions of snakes to eat the frogs, I really will bolt," I warned. "And I'm not coming back."

"Same here," Agnes agreed.

I finally got tired of watching frogs flood my hometown and sat at the table where Yngvarr was valiantly attempting to complete the *New York Times* crossword puzzle. Really, what else could we do? The city was completely shut down, and even the employees in this hotel had left, allowing us to stay behind so we could somehow combat a handful of gods who'd decided to inflict a little historical irony on us. Agnes had already studied all of the information different government agencies had collected on the rivers—because it hadn't been only the Mississippi River that turned to blood, but every river and tributary that ran through Baton Rouge—and the eyewitness accounts were first reported over forty-eight hours ago.

We'd been on the levee when the frog infestation began, almost twenty-four hours ago, so we—and by "we" I mean Agnes—assumed the Sumerians and Egyptians planned to unleash one plague on the city each day. And our time was almost up before the next plague hit.

"How many people are left in the city?" Keira asked.

"A few thousand, most of whom refused to leave," Agnes answered. "But there are also patients too critical to move, including Tyr."

"And clearly, those who *want* to leave are having a difficult time getting out," I added, gesturing to the gridlock that had traffic at a standstill.

"Right," Agnes sighed. "I guess if we include all the people trying to get out of Baton Rouge, that number is much higher. And they're all trapped."

Honestly, I'd never felt so helpless in my life. Sure, I was new at this heroics stuff, but when the next plague hit, how were we going to save all those people stuck in their vehicles, people who'd only been obeying the evacuation order? Unfortunately, no one had really been able to plan for just how difficult it would be to drive down interstates and highways filled with bullfrogs the size of pancakes.

"Time's up," Nuada murmured.

Joachim had been reading a heavily researched and brilliantly written book on the original plagues of Egypt—okay, he'd been reading the Gideon Bible he'd pulled from the nightstand—and even though we'd already made a list of each plague and what it might mean for Baton Rouge, he slowly made his way to the window and announced, "Biting insects. They won't necessarily be the same as the fleas or lice of Egypt though."

I groaned and cursed every Sumerian and Egyptian god I could remember, especially Ra, even though he was one of our allies. But since he wasn't in the room with us, I threw his name in there, too. "It's going to be mosquitoes," I said. "We already have a plague of mosquitoes."

As if to agree with me, the buzzing of wings filled the air, and I instinctively backed away from the window. Ever have a mosquito fly right next to your ear, and you kinda jump and swat at your head like a lunatic? Multiply that by a billion, and that's what the city was like. So many mosquitoes suddenly descended on Baton Rouge, the sky actually darkened, and as they swarmed lower to the ground, they obscured my view of the parked cars on the interstate.

The frogs had a brief moment to enjoy the feast before succumbing to the swarms. Yeah, there were so many mosquitoes the frogs literally died from blood loss. *From mosquitoes.* And those were obviously cold-blooded animals, which meant any warm-blooded animal or human out there didn't stand a chance.

"I'm not leaving this room," Agnes said, her eyes wide as she stared into the swirling black mass. "Ever."

"Well, I guess the good news is that they'll take care of the frog infestation," I said.

"Who's going to take care of the mosquito infestation?" Keira asked.

"Is there seriously no god who can magically kill bugs?" I asked back.

Yngvarr grabbed his tablet and tapped at the screen, so I gaped at him for a few seconds before snapping, "Are you seriously looking up gods who can magically kill bugs?"

He shook his head without looking up from the screen. "No. I'm looking up what repels them."

I scoffed and crossed my arms, a little relieved that someone else was finally acting like the village idiot. "Yeah, we'll just light a citronella candle and they'll fly away."

But Yngvarr was undeterred. He called Frey and asked him to join us, and he arrived with his sister, which made Keira a little defensive but I pretended not to notice. I'd learned by now this wasn't all about me. Keira and Freyja had a long history that had always been somewhat contentious, but I couldn't help feeling like it was my fault for giving into Freyja's flirting.

"New plan," Frey said. "We go back to Asgard and stay there. Baton Rouge is declared uninhabitable and burned to the ground, because really, fire's the only way to ensure these supernatural mosquitoes die."

"How do you know they're supernatural mosquitoes and not the regular kind?" I asked.

Frey pointed out the window and answered, "They've literally killed animals by draining them of blood. How is that even possible?"

I thought about it for a few seconds then nodded. "Good point."

"Frey," Yngvarr interjected, "let's try something. I have a list of plants that naturally repel mosquitoes. Can you make these grow all over the city?"

Frey read over the list and lifted a shoulder. "I *could* if I had seeds for all of these. Of course, even if I did, how would I get them on the ground?"

"I can do it," Keira said. "I'll get my horse and we'll fly above the swarms and drop them."

"No," I insisted. "I don't want you out there."

Keira touched my arm and met my eyes, which only strengthened my resistance to her leaving the safety of this room. "I'll ask the other Valkyries to help, and we'll spread out. I'll be back soon."

And really, there wasn't a damn thing I could do to stop her, so I impulsively pulled her closer and kissed her, not like the time we'd kissed in Reykjavik but in a "God, I hope you're not about to die" kind of way. Keira pulled away from me, surprised rather than angry, but whatever she wanted to tell me was interrupted when Nuada gestured to the window and said, "Something strange is happening out there."

So of course we all rushed to the window and discovered the something strange was the behavior of those mosquitoes. They'd descended on the carpet of frogs, obscuring the amphibians from our view, but now, the swarms were forming black tornadoes, leaving patches of ground visible between them. That's not technically true. I still couldn't see the ground, only dead bullfrogs. "What the hell?" Frey murmured.

I was pretty sure that was a rhetorical, "What the hell?" but I answered him anyway. "They killed all the frogs, so they're looking for something that's still alive."

"How much blood can one mosquito hold anyway?" Keira asked. That was probably another rhetorical question, but I answered her, too.

"These aren't Earth mosquitoes. Whoever created them probably ensured they had the capacity to drain a human."

Nuada glanced at me before returning his attention to the vortices of mosquitoes below. "I've never heard of a god that can create life from nothing. Not a god like *us*, I mean."

"Can y'all change it then?" I asked. "Take billions of larvae or whatever and make them different than normal?"

He nodded but kept his eyes trained on the ground. "*That* we can do. I'm a little disturbed that our enemies had billions of larvae at their disposal though. Why would anyone keep billions and billions of mosquito larvae on hand?"

I was about to agree with him, but I noticed something moving through the pulsing black masses below. The funnel clouds broke apart as an eight-foot alligator charged through them—if you've never seen an alligator up close, they're frighteningly fast—its mouth open as if it wanted to swallow the insects buzzing around its head. But from the opposite direction, another alligator charged through the clouds of mosquitoes, this one equally large and equally fast. They snapped at each other, and while I stood there wondering why the hell a couple of alligators would decide to brawl in the middle of a Biblical apocalypse, three more emerged from the swarms, breaking them apart and revealing more of the blanket of dead frogs.

"Um…" I stammered. "I don't remember alligator invasions being one of the plagues."

"Wild animals overrunning Egypt," Yngvarr said. "Yeah, this could be a bigger problem than the mosquitoes."

"If that's what's happening, if wild animals are overrunning Baton Rouge," Joachim said, "then the Sumerians are speeding up the plagues. They sent two at once."

"Shit," I sighed. And since Baton Rouge had become the new Sumerian labyrinth where just *thinking* something could make it happen and that something would most likely try to kill us, the sea of insects mostly dissipated, revealing a hellish landscape of dead animals and worse, live ones fighting and biting and clawing one another. Because it wasn't just alligators out there: wild boars, bears, and bobcats clashed, but they didn't seem content with just fighting each other. They were attacking the cars on the roadways, trying to get to the people trapped inside.

"We have to help them," Keira cried, grabbing my arm and dragging me toward the door.

"Wait," I insisted. "Don't you think it's suspicious that the mosquitoes are leaving now that warm-blooded animals have shown up? It's like they *wanted* us to see the deadly animals out there, and they *wanted* us to feel like we could step outside to fight."

"This whole city is one big trap," Frey argued. "But those people are going to die if we don't do something."

As if hearing Frey's warning, gunshots mixed with the sounds of bobcats screaming. But there was no way the people trapped along Baton Rouge's roadways had enough bullets to put down all the animals out there. And there were definitely too few of us to make much difference to the thousands trapped within the city. "Maybe we can at least clear the interstates," I suggested. "Get traffic moving again, let people get out."

Frey nodded thoughtfully and agreed, but honestly, I wasn't looking forward to fighting supernaturally-charged animals. That usually resulted in attempted dismemberment of limbs I'd rather stay attached to our bodies. Agnes stopped by the Egyptians' room and told Ra and Anubis what we were attempting, and they quickly offered to help us. I scowled at Ra for no other reason than he ended up walking too closely to Keira, even though he talked to Agnes the entire time.

In the lobby, we hesitated by the glass doors, mostly because there were four huge alligators right outside. Anubis tapped his chin as he stared at them then shrugged and said, "Bullets should work on them, right? They might be cursed animals, but they're not gods."

"Cursed," Ra murmured. He tapped *his* chin now as he studied the reptiles, which must have sent out some warning signal to the others since they were getting company. Those four alligators had multiplied to eight, and there were more on the way. "Perhaps we can save the entire city without slaughtering all these animals if we can figure out how to lift the curse."

"Lifting curses isn't in my repertoire of hero abilities," I said.

"What is?" Keira asked a little *too* quickly.

So, naturally, I just as quickly replied, "Let's go back to my room and I'll show you."

Surprisingly, she didn't hit me. Not surprisingly, she *did* roll her eyes and turned her attention back to Ra. "Odin does spells. Maybe—"

"Not him," Agnes and I interrupted at the same time.

Keira gave us a strange look, but Ra hardly noticed. He was still watching the *National Geographic* melee outside. He tilted his head and sighed. "Old friend, you know who could help us."

Anubis shook his head. "Not her. She can't be trusted."

Ra shrugged. "She could release these animals from their spell."

"At what cost?" Anubis demanded.

"Who?" Keira and I both asked. I didn't like the idea of owing anyone anything. I mean, if the only reason this mystery goddess would agree to save lives was to get something out of it for herself, she wasn't really any better than the gods trying to kill us with wild animals in the first place.

Ra gave us a quick glance and sighed. "Isis."

"You don't exactly have the best history with her," Anubis said. "I'll see if I can bring her back."

While Anubis went back to whatever world the Egyptian gods normally inhabited, I searched Havard's knowledge base, which was now sort of *my* knowledge base, for the history between Isis and Ra. But the only story he knew about them was something about Isis creating a super venomous snake that poisoned Ra, and she refused to help him until he told her his *real* name, which somehow made her more powerful.

And naturally, that made me want to know his real name. "Dude," I whispered. "What's your real name?"

He blinked at me while Agnes reminded him to ignore me.

"What if I guess it," I continued. "If I guess correctly, will that make me more powerful?"

When he didn't answer, I started guessing anyway. "Rumpelstiltskin?"

Nothing. Not even a smile. Keira, on the other hand, dragged me to the other side of the lobby, like that was going to stop me. "Keyser Söze?" I shouted to the Egyptian god who was desperately trying to pretend like I didn't exist.

"Gavyn, knock it off," Keira hissed.

I had no intention of stopping, but Anubis returned with a strikingly gorgeous woman with sleek dark hair and heavy bangs and an apparent fondness for gold jewelry that rivaled Freyja's. And Freyja must've noticed, too, because she looked the new goddess over with equal parts jealousy and rivalry.

"Didn't I tell you already I want no part of your quest to save this world?" she asked Ra. "These mortals no longer believe in us, so why should we care?"

"Well, she's delightful," I said loud enough for her to hear.

Isis squinted in my direction, but I really wasn't important enough for her to bother responding. I had the feeling when she looked at me, she only saw a gnat and would just as soon swat me away if I became too much of a nuisance.

"But you still care about wild animals," Ra offered. "Lift this curse and take as many home with you as you want."

Isis squeezed past him to look out the glass doors. She tossed that impossibly smooth hair over a shoulder and after a couple of tense, heavy minutes, said, "I'll take those cats," referring to the bobcats and a larger cat I hadn't seen before and thought didn't even *live* in this area anymore. But when I heard what sounded like multiple women loudly screaming, I knew cougars had returned to Louisiana.

She cracked the door open and slipped outside, and my mouth fell open as I watched the goddess step into an actual alligator brawl. My first thought was that she was obviously crazy and I was about to watch her get torn into little pieces of alligator food. But when the reptiles didn't touch her—and even stopped fighting and relaxed in her presence, turning into the largely immobile living logs I was used to seeing in zoos—I realized she was putting her own spell on them to calm the wild beasts and make them harmless.

Only the cats still moved, but they were no longer screaming or fighting. They ran to gather near her and when she was satisfied with the number of felines she'd be taking home for her own personal supernatural zoo, she waved a hand at them and they disappeared.

"What the—" I mumbled, but Ra answered me before I could finish.

"She just crossed the veil. The remaining animals are subdued and pose no threat to us or the people still trapped in the city."

I eyed the alligators warily. I didn't care what he claimed: being eaten by an eight-foot gator was *not* an acceptable way to die.

"Anybody remember what the next plague is?" Joachim

asked carefully. He was watching the largely immobile animals outside like he completely agreed with me.

"Yeah," Anubis answered. "And if they're sticking to the script, this isn't going to be pretty."

I was a second away from insisting I wasn't lancing any boils when Keira stepped closer to the glass door and said, "Are these animals still alive?"

"Isis *loves* animals. She wouldn't have killed them," Ra said.

"I don't think she did," Nuada offered. "I think it's the next plague."

I didn't remember any sudden animal deaths as one of the plagues, but Frey opened the door and slowly crouched beside one of the now completely still alligators. He reached a hesitant hand toward it and part of me wanted to shout, "Gotcha!" as soon as his fingers brushed against the tough skin, but I hurried to his side instead, sword ready in case I needed to lob off its head when it tried to eat my friend.

But as Frey's hand touched the dark green back of the gator, I noticed Keira was right. None of these animals—even the mammals like the boars and remaining cats—were breathing. They'd all relaxed and lain down when her spell covered the city, but they'd clearly been sleeping. Something had suddenly killed them.

"Disease," Anubis breathed beside me. "It affected livestock, which meant people lost their milk and meat supplies. This time, it's obviously affecting *all* animals."

"Bastards," I muttered. I assumed those who'd been lucky enough to get out of Baton Rouge had at least taken their pets with them, but this city was about to become an enormous pet cemetery. And I'd read that book: no way did I want to spend one more night here.

As if reading my mind, Agnes gestured to the horizon and said, "Sun's setting. I don't think we should roam the streets after dark. The people who are trapped here may become as dangerous as the plagues themselves. And that's the third plague to hit in one day. They may unleash more overnight."

I kicked a desiccated frog away from my foot and wrinkled my nose. Between the rivers of blood and amphibian guts on all the roadways, Baton Rouge already smelled like the massive animal grave it was about to become.

"We can't fight magic," I said. "There's really nothing we can do for this city."

"I know," Frey agreed. "But I can't abandon it either. I don't want to be the kind of god who would just leave people to suffer."

Yngvarr nodded and put a hand on my shoulder. "Come on. I'll raid the bar with you."

I tried to offer him a grateful smile, but knowing what was happening to my hometown and knowing what was still to come, that smile never reached my lips. Each of us knew the sun rising in the morning wouldn't bring the hope of a new day, but the horrors of a past that we couldn't combat. And for the first time since this war with the Sumerians began, we could very likely fail.

CHAPTER EIGHT

The morning light revealed a city filled with the slowly rotting corpses of animals and the overpowering stench you'd expect with dead bodies everywhere. Flies had replaced the mosquito swarms from the day before, but as we slowly wove our way through buzzing carcasses, pressing hotel hand towels over our mouths and noses in a futile attempt to block some of the smell, I concluded these were the normal, regular flies that were always attracted to dead bodies. Mostly because there weren't nearly as many of them as the mosquito invasion.

"I think I'm going to throw up," Yngvarr mumbled into his towel.

I nodded and searched for a patch of pavement to step on. Those empty spaces were few and far between the bodies. We'd set out this morning more than a little concerned that we couldn't see anyone in their vehicles anymore. But our hopes that everyone was still sleeping were dashed when Frey reached a car and peered through a window.

"Empty," he shouted back to us.

Nuada and Agnes stepped over a dead alligator to reach a truck with its windows rolled down. "Also empty," she said.

I let my hand clutching the white hand towel drop and asked, "Where the hell is everyone?" I didn't expect any of my allies to have an answer, but no one had come to the hotel overnight, which would have been the most logical place to seek shelter. But Frey leaned closer to the car then let his own towel fall as he pulled the door open.

"I think I know where they're going," he said.

I stepped up to the car, careful to avoid the bloated boar near the front tire, and peeked inside. I instinctively covered my mouth and nose again, even though the inside of the car didn't really smell worse than the air outside. But the upholstery of the seats was covered in blood and something that had dried to a nauseating yellowish-brown.

"What *is* that?" I groaned.

Frey jabbed it with the tip of his sword like it might come alive and attack us. "Um... I think it's blood and pus. And I think the next plague began overnight, just as we'd feared."

I glanced over my shoulder toward Keira who looked even paler than usual, but it was Ra who lost his breakfast. He turned away from the vehicles and retched into a ditch, and I'm not gonna lie, I felt a little better about the guy after that. I mean, what were the chances Keira would still find him irresistibly sexy after seeing him empty his stomach into a ditch?

"Boils," Joachim said. "They must have gone to the closest hospital."

"Only a handful of personnel stayed behind," Agnes said. "We can at least get over there and help them keep order until everyone can be treated."

But Keira touched my arm to get my attention. "Do you know what causes boils?"

I had no idea, actually. I wasn't even sure what boils *were*.

"Usually, it's a strain of staph, the kind that even without supernatural intervention has become extremely difficult to treat. It's been less than twenty-four hours and sores are rupturing and bleeding. That shouldn't happen, Gavyn."

Admittedly, my first thought was something along the lines of, "How can any woman be so beautiful *and* smart?" but my second, at least, was more appropriate and along the lines of, "If that's true, then there's not a damn thing we can do to save those people." And I said *that* one out loud since it seemed a hell of a lot more relevant than admiring her beauty and intelligence once again.

"You're right," Keira said. "The only way we can help these people is by killing the god controlling the magic."

"We'll split up," Anubis suggested. "Even if Asalluhi has company, we should outnumber them."

I wondered if he'd ever encountered Asalluhi before. Every experience from the Sumerian labyrinth was still painfully fresh in my mind, and I didn't like the idea of having even one less god or hero at my side if we were able to fight this god of magic once and for all.

"Call the others," Agnes suggested. "Rather than splitting up, let's all meet somewhere and search for Asalluhi together."

Apparently, those memories were still haunting Agnes, too.

The others she'd mentioned included Freyja, who'd remained inside the hotel, and Thor, a few of our heroes, and Enki and Ninhursag, all of whom had decided to stay at a different hotel on the other side of the city so we'd be at both ends and better able to respond to emergencies. But despite our intentions, we hadn't been prepared for the assaults this city would face. I mean, how is anyone supposed to fight boils or some mysterious disease afflicting all of the animals here?

"Gavyn, you know this city. Where should we meet them?" Keira asked.

"The Marriott off College. They can't miss it. It's the tallest building in the area."

Yngvarr relayed our message then we spent a good five minutes arguing about the best way to get into the heart of the city. Between the carrion littering the streets and the abandoned vehicles clogging the parts of roads not covered by buzzard-breakfast, driving seemed out of the question. But walking would take hours these sick people didn't have.

Ra, who still looked a bit seasick even though he'd emptied his stomach, finally interrupted our arguing by saying, "What if we find a vehicle that's capable of driving off-road and over piles of animal bodies?"

I folded my arms over my chest and snapped, "If it's a vehicle capable of driving off-road, why wouldn't its owners have gotten off the streets and escaped?"

Ra shrugged. "They were caught in bumper-to-bumper traffic. We can move cars out of the way, though."

I scrambled for another reason to claim his idea was completely stupid, but really, it was a completely obvious solution, and I suspected my friends all felt like they'd joined me as the village idiot. We found a Chevy Colorado and managed to get it off the road. Agnes wanted to drive, so I announced I was walking after all, but Nuada tossed me the keys. Only Keira sat in the cab with me while everyone else piled into the bed and found something to hang onto. Above us, black birds—most likely vultures—circled, waiting for us to leave since we'd disrupted their feast.

"Ever seen anything like this?" I asked her.

"No. But I've encountered magic before, and you need to be careful here. Asalluhi can turn even the familiar into something foreign."

I'd just begun the bumpy drive into the heart of the city

with a handful of gods and a hero in the back yelling at me to slow down because they were getting tossed around like bingo balls, so naturally, I sped up a little. Now, I'd grown up here, and while I'd never stayed at the Marriott, I knew exactly how to get to that area of the city because it just happened to be near a Hooters, which Hunter and I *may* have gone to once or twice. But as I turned onto a familiar street—or, more accurately, the sidewalk—Keira's prediction came true. I wasn't on Lee Drive at all.

I wasn't actually sure *where* we'd ended up, but it wasn't my Baton Rouge. The buildings were too close to the street and impossibly tall, and this city didn't have skyscrapers. But I was forced back to the road since the buildings sprouted next to the asphalt. And I realized there wasn't a single stalled car blocking my way.

I took my foot off the gas and glanced at Keira. "I don't like this. What should we do?"

She looked over her shoulder and gasped, so I put the truck in park and looked, too. We couldn't have gone more than a few hundred feet since turning, but what was supposed to be Lee Drive stretched endlessly behind us, the tall metal and glass buildings peeking into the heavens and the suspiciously clear road disappearing into the horizon. I tapped on the glass between the cab and bed to get Agnes's attention and slid the window open. "Which way on Elm Street?" I asked.

"Elm?" she repeated. "Are we on Elm? And why would I know which way to go?"

"Seriously, Agnes. Watch a few movies every now and then. What else do you have to do with your immortal existence?"

Frey leaned over and whispered in her ear then Agnes grunted at me when she finally understood the reference to being on Elm Street.

"I don't think it matters which direction we choose anyway," Yngvarr offered.

"It did in the labyrinth," Joachim argued. "Even when we all got turned around, Enki and Ninhursag kept their bearings because they knew their city so well. Just keep going as if everything looked normal. Turn when you think you should."

"Into a building?" I snapped.

"Maybe slow down first," Ra joked.

I sighed and turned around again. Just parking here and doing nothing didn't seem like a good option either, so I put the truck back in drive and made it all of five hundred feet when the damn thing just quit. No warning. No sputtering or smoking from the engine. It had half a tank of gas. But it just *stopped*.

I stared at the dashboard for a few seconds then at Keira for a few more seconds before wisely announcing, "This doesn't bode well for us."

Agnes poked her head through the open window and glanced between us then scowled at the dashboard, so I suggested, "Try scowling as the old witch. Maybe you can scare the truck into running."

"I think we're walking," she said instead.

As we piled out of the now dead truck, Yngvarr called Thor, and none of us were really surprised to learn they were having similar problems getting to our rendezvous point. Yngvarr had the call on speaker, so when Thor asked if we'd tried going into one of the buildings yet, I immediately approached one... only to discover I couldn't find the door.

"Um... how?" I yelled over my shoulder.

"Exactly," he said.

"Can you break into it?" Agnes asked.

"Already tried," Thor said. "And if I can't get into it with Mjollnir, I don't see how it can be done."

"So indestructible glass," I complained. "What the hell is the point of having all these buildings if we can't get inside?"

Frey's eyes widened, and he grabbed my arm. "To taunt us."

So I looked him over quickly then shook my head. "Dude, *you* may feel threatened by the undeniably phallic shaped skyscrapers, but—"

"No," he interrupted. "The next plague. We'll be surrounded by shelter that we can't actually use. *That's* the point. We can't get off this street, and we can't find cover."

I was still rifling through my sluggish mental catalogue, trying to remember what the next plague was and why it worried Frey so much, when the first bright streak lit up the sky in the east. I hadn't even noticed the sky darkening like a thunderstorm was rolling in, but when I followed the fire across the sky, I would've sworn it was twilight even though I knew better. It couldn't even be noon yet.

"Fiery hail," I breathed. Of course, it couldn't actually be hail… fiery chunks of ice just didn't make sense, but meteorites? Charcoal? Hell, we weren't sure what the fire falling from the sky actually was, but it didn't really matter. It had begun to fall, and if we didn't find cover soon, we'd be stuck in a deadly hailstorm.

"My shield!" I yelled, holding it above our heads as several more brilliant streaks of orange lit up the sky. "Everyone who can't fit into the cab of the truck can hide beneath it."

I tried to convince Keira to get inside the truck, but she refused to leave my side. We ended up forcing Ra, Anubis, and Yngvarr into it while the rest of us huddled uncomfortably close, hoping the enchantment of the shield would extend far enough to protect us. Yngvarr was still arguing with Agnes, since he wanted her inside the truck as well, insisting she could sit on his lap, so I told him now wasn't the time for lap dances and added, "You perv," for good measure.

A fiery ball of *something* whistled toward us and hit my shield with so much force, it knocked me into the side of the truck. I managed to hold onto the shield, but the sky had lit up like the Fourth of July and Agnes's feeble argument that she didn't want to risk opening the sutures on Yngvarr's leg seemed trite compared to the literal firestorm that was seconds away. "Grab her!" I shouted at Yngvarr, pushing her toward him while trying to keep my shield positioned above the rest of us.

Agnes still protested, but we were out of time to argue about it. The fake street ignited in a brilliant display of yellows and oranges and reds as the fiery hail pelted the earth, occasionally opening craters in the street that smoldered, sending gray and blue swirls of ash and smoke into the air. One of the meteorites, or whatever these deadly projectiles were, hit the roof of the truck, causing a huge indentation. I wasn't sure how it didn't burst through and could only assume one of the gods inside was using whatever power they had to fortify the truck.

Honestly, I still wasn't sure what kind of power war gods or goddesses possessed, so being able to turn an ordinary truck into an actual fortress seemed as good as any.

I first noticed the black fingers reaching into the sky as Nuada, Frey, Keira, and I huddled beneath a shield that was really too small to protect all of us. The buildings surrounding us obscured most of our views, but between them, there were narrow strips of unobstructed sky… and Baton Rouge was burning.

"Oh, my God," I groaned. "The whole city will be destroyed."

As if hearing me, two things happened at once: Agnes's phone began to ring, or more accurately, playing a song by Hozier, the popular Irish folk rock musician. I'd been meaning to ask my Norse friends if they had popular Norwegian music as their ringtones, but I doubted popular Norwegian music even existed.

The second thing that happened at the same time Hozier began serenading us was that rain mixed with the fiery hail. But not just a drizzle. The sky exploded and rain fell so thickly, we could no longer see beyond the edges of the shield I kept over us. I suspected the rain was Thor's solution to the fires spreading all over the city, and I'd later learn I was right, but unfortunately, it couldn't stop the fiery hail still punishing Baton Rouge for a sin it had never committed.

And while Thor's plan to prevent the city from burning to the ground worked, it didn't take long to figure out it would come at a price. The water rose above our ankles, and still, the fire fell from the sky, so the rain continued to follow. I kinda thought nothing could catch on fire at this point, but I'd also never dealt with supernatural firebombs, so what did I know?

As the water continued to rise and the fiery hail continued to fall, I realized something else: the water would fill the cab of the truck, which meant we'd lose the only source of protection we had against the hail except for my shield. I was still trying to puzzle through how we could survive two sort-of natural disasters when I first heard the scream. High-pitched and shrill, it somehow cut through the overwhelming noise of the unyielding rain and the constant impacts of destructive, blazing hail the size of baseballs.

My fear that I was losing my mind, what little mind I had, was quickly calmed when the scream echoed down the odd street again, and this time, Keira inhaled sharply and clutched the back of my shirt. "It sounds like a child," she cried.

"It has to be a trap," I countered. I mean, what were the chances a child was wandering around the streets of Baton Rouge, especially *this* nightmarish street that didn't actually exist?

Ultimately, it didn't matter if the child were real or not. A distorted figure appeared at the far end of the street where Lee High should have been, but instead, only more of the identical, doorless and windowless buildings stretched lazily into the inferno above us. And Keira, being my brave and selfless Valkyrie with the permanent longing for the one thing she could never have, darted away from me and half-ran, half-swam toward the toddling, falling apparition.

And, of course, I couldn't let Keira go without me. I shoved my shield toward Frey and followed her, just as the rising floodwaters—which were rising *preternaturally* fast, I might add—formed waves that kept knocking us face-first into what had become a river. The child, if it was a real child, was knocked down, and she tried to scream again but was covered by the wave. Keira screamed, too, and swam faster.

My heart leapt into my ears and its beating was all I could hear now. Whether that little girl was real or not, she *looked* real, and I couldn't stomach the thought of watching a child drown. I fought against the waves that fought back, but our one advantage was that they should be moving the child toward us.

But she hadn't reemerged since being dragged beneath the surface of the water.

So I took a deep breath and dove in. Because the day any of us stopped risking our lives for even the *possibility* that we were saving a child's life would be the day the Sumerians won after all.

CHAPTER NINE

Too much time. Too much time.

The seconds kept ticking off the clock, and with each imaginary click of my mental stopwatch, I just knew this little girl, if she were real, would die and I'd fail in my most important battle yet. Keira kept pace with me as we fought the increasingly powerful currents. Sure, our demigod genes gave us an advantage over ordinary humans, but we obviously weren't invincible. The struggle was taking a toll on us both.

I was beginning to give up hope when my fingers brushed against something as it shot past me, caught in one of the powerful currents of this new river. I had to stop swimming and allow the water to sweep me away, too, so I could try to grab onto whatever had just passed me. This time, as I glimpsed the dark outline of what may have been a child, I was ready. I hooked my arm around her and pushed off the street toward the surface.

As I gasped for air, Keira grabbed me and dragged us toward one of the useless buildings. I'd been in this situation before: narrow street, tidal wave submerging us. Yeah, the six feet of water trying to drown us now wasn't Thor's doing.

Keira was looking for something to hold onto, but these buildings hadn't become less useless all of a sudden.

"Give her to me," she shouted over the rain and crashing waves.

For the first time, I actually looked at what I'd just scooped from the water. A small, elfin face with groggy eyes and dark hair plastered to pale cheeks, arms still bearing the plumpness from toddlerhood. How old could she be? Three? As Keira wrapped an arm around her, the little girl's eyes fluttered and fixed on Keira's face, and she seemed to remember where she was. She whimpered and clung tightly to Keira's neck, but my Valkyrie didn't loosen the girl's death grip. Instead, she nodded toward the truck and asked me to steer us all there.

We were halfway back when I realized the fiery hail had stopped. Seconds later, the rain stopped, too. I let the currents carry us to our friends, only occasionally steering us back on course, but I was exhausted. As we neared the truck, Ra and Agnes dove into the water to pull us the rest of the way. Most of the vehicle was submerged, but at least it gave us something to cling to.

Knowing Keira must be exhausted as well, Agnes tried to coax the child from her, but the more Agnes tried to get her away from Keira, the tighter the child held on. Not that I blamed her. I wouldn't let a witch grab me either. But Keira looked like she didn't want to let go either. She murmured softly to the child, who'd begun to cry, and sang a sweet lullaby Havard must have known, too, because I recognized it even though she wasn't singing in English.

"So," I said. "The Sumerians have decided to amp up their timeline. These plagues definitely aren't being spaced out by twenty-four hours anymore. Hell, they're not even a few hours apart sometimes."

Anubis nodded. "And all our phones got soaked. We can't reach Thor or anyone else, for that matter."

The water drained as quickly as it had risen, although I wasn't really sure *where* all this water was going. I was a little more sure that we were about to get hit with the next plague, but Agnes wasn't convinced.

"It could be Enki controlling the water," she argued. "We should still try to reach them."

"How?" I asked. "This street doesn't exist, and we have a traumatized preschooler. And what is the next plague, anyway?"

"Locusts," Yngvarr said.

"Locusts," I repeated. "Like grasshoppers?"

"Exactly like grasshoppers. Only millions of them. And that's when swarms occur naturally. But supernatural swarms? Who knows how many locusts will be in them."

I rubbed my tired eyes and sighed. "Okay, so aside from a sudden soy bean and sugar cane shortage, what's the danger to humans?"

"I've seen the way you Americans eat," Joachim said. "A sugar shortage seems pretty serious."

"If millions of grasshoppers can devastate entire fields of crops, imagine the magnitude of Asalluhi's swarm," Anubis said.

"We need to get off this street," I decided.

For once, everyone agreed with me, but there didn't appear to *be* a way off the street. It stretched into the distance in both directions, tall buildings blocking our view or escape on either side. The space between the buildings, which I was certain had existed before, suddenly *didn't*. It was like the skyscrapers just decided to scrape against each other, too, blocking any exit we might find that way. And that meant we were forced to walk on the street, along the path the Sumerian god of magic obviously wanted us to take.

The child Keira carried had quieted, but her eyes remained wide and had settled on me, so I smiled at her and told her I was from Baton Rouge, too. I asked her if she liked Mike the Tiger—because what child grew up around here and *didn't* like LSU's mascot?—and she smiled back at me but didn't answer. I wondered, of course, as I'm sure we all did, how she'd become separated from her family and if her parents were even still alive. Ninurta had once drawn the line at massacring children when he'd been in his televised destruction phase, but that didn't mean *all* gods shared his reservations. Maybe this poor girl was somehow a trap, too, like they'd put a bomb in her or something.

Okay, maybe not a bomb, but come on—you're also thinking it's strange that a small child just wandered into a cursed street with us, right? I suspected Asalluhi knew we'd never leave her behind, and he hoped she'd slow us down or even divert our attention altogether.

Since city blocks no longer existed, I couldn't really tell how far we'd gone when we first heard the swarm. And even though I knew locusts were grasshoppers, they sounded just like wasps... huge, angry, deadly wasps. We all froze and looked around, but the street remained as never-ending and the buildings as unyielding. "Maybe," I said, "they won't be able to reach us."

Agnes slapped my shoulder as soon as the words finished tumbling from my stupid mouth, and sure enough, the waspy buzzing grew louder as the first grasshoppers spilled onto the street. The child lifted her head and screamed as large brown and green and tan insects the size of a roll of pennies flapped against our skin and landed in our hair.

And that's when the first one of those bastards *bit me*.

"Son of a *bitch*!" I yelled, swatting at the miniature demon.

Keira had dropped to the ground, using her body to shield the child, and without thinking, I pulled my shirt off and covered one side of the child's exposed arms and legs. In my peripheral vision, I noticed Joachim and Ra doing the same, and soon, all of the guys had stripped off their shirts in an effort to insulate this poor girl from the admittedly painful bites of *grasshoppers*.

I grew up in south Louisiana. These insects were no strangers to me; in fact, I'd often come across these massive black swamp grasshoppers that could easily grow to the size of an adult woman's hand. My friends and I used to catch them and put them in jars, but we'd always let them out when we were done playing. And yet, not one of them had ever *bitten me*.

All we could do now was hastily swat at the locusts as they landed on someone's skin, but our backs were already becoming bloody minefields, and I was clearly flirting with hysterics as I thought we could now play connect the dots if we had a permanent marker. Okay, that's not the whole truth: the part that made me think I was beginning to flirt with insanity may have something to do with my increasingly real belief that by connecting the dots, we'd create a map out of this cursed part of the city.

Fortunately, I was too busy keeping swarms of grasshoppers off my friends to vocalize my now utter conviction that our salvation lay in the bloody patchworks of our skin.

I'd been so preoccupied, I hadn't noticed Agnes and Ra running in the opposite direction, back toward the now useless truck. By the time I realized they were gone, I heard the screeching of metal and waved my shield frantically in front of me to clear a line of sight toward them. They'd ripped the hood off, and Ra began running back to us while Agnes jumped into the bed of the truck and began tearing off the tailgate and roof of the cab. I was more than a little impressed by her strength, but mostly, I was just confused as hell.

"Shelter," he yelled. "Everyone on the ground, as closely as possible."

I mean... *seriously*? A hood, a tailgate, and a roof? That was going to take some *serious* magic to protect seven adults and a small child from a pervasive, aggressive swarm of nasty locusts.

But then again, I *had* apparently forgotten most of my companions *were* gods. And while they may not be gods of magic like Asalluhi, they still had quite a few tricks up their sleeves. Well, not literally, considering all the guys had taken off their shirts to protect the child, but you know what I mean.

We crouched beneath the sheets of metal, and I used my shield to plug the largest gap. Ra placed both palms on the asphalt and took a deep breath. "Are you ready?"

Who the hell was he asking?

"Um... ready for what?" I asked.

"Just stay inside our... fort. We'll be safe here."

Considering those damn grasshoppers were still getting in through all the cracks, I sincerely doubted this guy understood the meaning of "safe," but the unmistakable sound of a fire erupting outside our pitiful fort and the equally unmistakable sounds of millions of little insect bodies getting charbroiled answered my question before I could even ask it.

"It'll get too hot in here—" I started, but Ra cut me off.

"We'll be fine. Besides, the locusts will move farther away from us to get away from the fires, and I'll just keep widening the circle."

We listened silently as the fire roared around us and the locusts sizzled and dropped into the flames, and soon, the street smelled like an odd cross between a barbecue and burning hair. I had no idea *why* it smelled like burning hair, but that was really at the bottom of my "What the hell?" list at the moment.

"Be careful," Anubis cautioned. "We can't risk this fire getting out of control and have no way of reaching Thor to get him to bring back the rain."

"I could go to Asgard and get…" Frey trailed off and his eyes narrowed in frustrated confusion. "The veil… I can't sense it anymore."

"They've shut us off. We're trapped, just like in Sumer II," Agnes said.

And thinking of Sumer II reminded me of an important, potentially life saving oversight. "Do you remember seeing any manhole covers?" I asked. "I'm pretty sure these locusts can't get down there."

"No," Frey sighed. "Just poison gas and devil dogs."

"Devil… what?" Anubis asked.

I waved him off, or at least tried to. I mean, we were pretty cramped in there. Then, I urged someone to help me find an entry point to whatever underground utilities were in this part of the city. I wasn't at all surprised when the first person to volunteer was Joachim. Keira returned our shirts in the hopes they'd provide a little more protection against the possessed grasshoppers then Joachim and I slipped between the hood and tailgate to begin our search for a possible escape. Ra had to let the ring of fire collapse long enough for us to get through, but as soon as we reached the other side, the flames leapt into the sky again.

Once we were out of earshot, he whispered, "Do you ever regret opening your door all those weeks ago?"

"Only every minute of every day."

"Yeah," he sighed while swinging his normal, unenchanted shield at the clouds of locusts trying to attach themselves to his face like a face-hugging Xenomorph. "I thought I was signing up for epic battles between heroes and gods, not monsters and mutants and floods and labyrinths."

"I didn't sign up for any of this, actually. Bastards kidnapped me."

Joachim snorted and pointed his bow toward the street. As I batted grasshoppers away with my own shield, I squinted at the metal disc and asked, "Does this look like it leads to a sewer?"

"How should I know? I'm not even from this country."

"You don't have sewers in Germany?"

"Help me open it," he sighed.

I imagined trying to open a heavy manhole cover without a crowbar was a pain in the ass under normal circumstances. But while being attacked by a zillion grasshoppers—give or take a few billion—it was damn near impossible. Every time we thought we had a halfway decent grip on it, one of us had to let go to scream, curse, and swat insects that I was becoming increasingly convinced really *were* Xenomorphs in disguise.

I looked over my shoulder to where the rest of our group remained hidden inside Ra's magical fire circle and realized one of us would have to run back to let everyone know we'd found an entrance to what I hoped wasn't a sewer. Joachim seemed to realize it at the same time, so he lifted the disc higher and nodded toward the ladder. "Climb down and be ready to push it open once we return."

I didn't like the looks of the rusty ladder *or* the dank smell wafting from whatever awaited me below, but it was likely our only chance to escape this particular *Nightmare on Elm Street*. For the record, I was really beginning to think I'd take my chances with Freddy Krueger. I slung my shield over my shoulder by the leather strap and sheathed my sword then descended into the total darkness below.

CHAPTER TEN

Ra was the last to join us beneath the cursed street since he was keeping the locusts away with fire. Apparently, one of the perks of being a sun god was an ability to concentrate the heat of the sun until a fire ignited, which was actually pretty cool... not that I'd ever admit that out loud.

But once we were below ground, there was no sun for him to draw power from, so we were basically blind. And the little girl whose name we still hadn't learned definitely didn't like the dark. She began screaming—this ear-splitting sound that echoed throughout the narrow tunnel. If there were any devil dogs or demigods down here, they knew *we* were here now, too.

Keira tried to comfort her, but the child refused to be consoled this time. In fact, the only thing that could possibly calm her down was not to be in pitch blackness with a bunch of strangers in a city being overrun by monsters. We could do nothing about most of those problems, but maybe someone's phone was at least functional enough that the flashlight worked.

We dug through pockets, procuring our most likely permanently incapacitated smartphones—I hadn't even paid mine off yet—then remembered one of the reasons it had been so damn expensive in the first place.

It was supposedly waterproof.

I was pretty sure the salesman told me to let it dry out before turning it back on, but I didn't have time to wait around on natural processes like absorption and evaporation.

See? I know things.

I held the phone out in my palm and asked, "Any chance one of you gods has drying powers?"

"Drying... powers," Frey repeated slowly.

"Oh, I guess you can't see that I'm holding my Galaxy in my hand. But if we can dry it and get it working, we can call Thor *and* use it as a flashlight."

"Great idea, only I don't think 'drying powers' exist."

"Um..." one of the Egyptian gods stammered, but I didn't know which one. I hadn't really learned to distinguish their voices yet. "I might be able to help."

His feet shuffled against the floor as I directed him toward me with my voice then I placed my phone in his hands.

"Anubis?" Agnes said. "What are you doing?"

"Well, I had pretty specific connections to the mortal world," he answered carefully.

"You're going to bring my phone to the Land of the Electronic Dead?" I asked. "And is that Land only for smartphones or all electronics, because I had this *sweet* refurbished classic Nintendo, and—"

"Gavyn," Keira sighed over the child's screaming.

"Fine," I relented, but only because I wanted the child to stop screaming, too. "Are you going to resurrect my phone then?"

"No," Anubis said, still carefully measuring his words,

either because he thought we'd think he was nuts or because he thought *I* was nuts. "Part of being a god of the dead for the people of Egypt meant I was associated with their burial practices, too. They had to learn how to do the things I could do simply by touching a body."

I grunted impatiently toward the sound of his voice and snapped, "So you're mummifying my phone?"

"One of the first steps in mummification is drying out the skin. And I've already dried your phone." A bright narrow light broke through the complete darkness, and the girl *finally* stopped screaming. Her head whipped around, looking for the light's source, and when she spotted my cellphone, she reached for it, straining against Keira's arms. Anubis got that deer in the headlights look on his face, so I took my phone from him and gave it to the child so she wouldn't start screaming again.

But now that the girl was quiet, I turned back to Anubis and said, "You must be the *life* of the party."

I'm pretty sure even the little girl groaned.

"Walk," Agnes ordered, so I turned to *her* now and asked, "Is he the one who mummified you?"

Agnes arched an eyebrow at me and again ordered, "Walk."

"I have no idea *where* we're supposed to be walking," I pointed out.

"Our options are pretty limited," Yngvarr said. "I vote for going until we reach another ladder then checking for locusts. We only need to stay down here until the infestation is over."

"Then we might as well just stand here. If we end up going in the wrong direction, we'll end up farther from Thor and the others," I argued.

As logical as my argument was, for once, it quickly became apparent we *couldn't* just stand there waiting for the locusts to leave. Something flickered at the end of the tunnel where it turned, and I *wanted* to believe it was just an optical illusion, some trick of the flashlight that wouldn't stay still because the child herself seemed incapable of staying still, but when did our luck *ever* work that way?

"Did anybody else see something down there?" I asked quietly.

"Yep," Joachim said.

"Any clue what it was?"

"Nope."

"Think there's a chance it's *not* going to try to kill us?"

"Nope."

"I think we should walk in the opposite direction," Agnes said.

I was pretty sure that would mean walking *away* from the center of the city where we'd agreed to meet Thor and the others, but I was *definitely* sure I didn't want to find out if the weird, spectral shape we'd all apparently noticed was real. But since Asalluhi *was* an asshole and everything, he never gave us the choice. The clopping of hooved feet echoed down the tunnel, and it was like we were all stuck in slow motion as we turned toward the sound, wondering what horror was charging toward us.

I really shouldn't have wondered.

The creature rounded the corner, and the poor child screamed again and dropped my phone. I scrambled after it, but what looked an awful lot like the Minotaur's ghost was bearing down on us, and I really didn't want to find out if a phantom could gore me. My fingers wrapped around the smooth plastic case of my phone just as Yngvarr yanked on my other arm, pulling me to my feet and yelling at me to run. But my shield, which was still slung over a shoulder, hit me in the back of my head as I rose too quickly, and I had a better idea than reenacting the Running of the Bulls: Hell Edition.

Instead of running away from it, I ran *toward* it. Not

surprisingly, all of my allies shouted at me like I'd lost my mind, which was a definite possibility, but as I ran, I pulled my shield in front of me then dropped to a knee to brace myself for the impact... if one were possible. I mean, it *looked* like a ghost, so maybe it would just pass through me. And maybe we were all freaking out for nothing.

Turned out, there was an excellent reason we were all freaking out, and as the bull-man who must've been at *least* ten feet tall slammed into the enchantment of my shield, I fell on my ass and skidded a good thirty feet backwards. The bull-man shook his enormous bull-head as if clearing the stars from his vision then charged me again. I didn't have time to get on a knee again, so I just held my shield up and let the bastard run into me and send me scuttling across the tunnel floor.

"What the hell is this thing?" I yelled as he shook his head a second time. He wobbled a bit but clearly planned to keep charging me until one of us was dead.

"I think," Ra answered, "it's an Ekimmu."

The bull-man snorted at Ra and lowered his head, so I groaned and prepared for yet another painful impact. I couldn't keep doing this indefinitely. "And how do we kill it?" I yelled over my shoulder.

"That's kinda the problem," Ra said. "He's already dead."

I would've been a little more startled if I hadn't already fought demons and flaming zombie monkeys. But the damn bull-man ghost rammed me again, knocking me into a wall and knocking himself onto his back. Yngvarr and Frey used the all-too brief respite to help me on my feet, but I already felt like I'd been run over by a semi-truck. Actually, that wasn't too far from the truth.

The bull-man rolled over, forcing himself to his feet, so I grunted at him and complained, "Dude, *come on*! Just go on back to your pasture and find a nice little ghost cow to settle down with so—"

"Why little?" Yngvarr interrupted, like the size of the ghost cow mattered. "I don't think being little is a desirable trait among bovines."

I stared at him for a few seconds before saying, "You're putting way too much thought into what makes a cow attractive."

Apparently, the bull-man agreed. His large, dark eyes settled on Yngvarr, and he snorted and lowered his head, but Joachim decided arrows might be suitable ghost deterrents and unleashed an entire quiver full at our undead friend's head.

Not surprisingly, they didn't stop the Ekimmu, but they did seem to either confuse or annoy him. Each arrow that entered his head passed through it, but not before breaking apart some of the sickly green, ethereal mistiness that formed his body.

"The metals," Agnes exclaimed. "Iron and silver have all sorts of superstitions around them, including the ability to repel ghosts."

"And witches?" I asked, just to be a smartass, but she nodded and said, "Yeah, any malevolent creature."

She'd unsheathed her sword, but I didn't think it was a good idea for us to get that close to the ghastly bull-man. After all, Joachim had just shot a dozen arrows in the monster's head and it had only slowed him down.

"What if everyone shoots arrows at it?" I suggested.

Agnes shook her head, the stubborn old witch. "Not enough iron in the arrowheads. We need to attack him with our swords."

We were out of time anyway. The bull-man had completely reformed and was already running toward us. Fortunately, he didn't seem particularly smart, which was probably the only reason we survived. We waited until he'd rammed into my shield, dazing him once again, before falling on him with our swords, slashing and slicing wildly as we broke apart the odd, cloud-like substance that comprised his body.

He snorted and roared at us, because ghost bulls could apparently roar, but Agnes had been right once again. The amount of iron in our blades was too much for the phantom to handle. The bull-man finally broke apart and disappeared, but none of us believed this vanishing act would be permanent.

"Let's get out of this tunnel," Frey suggested.

I glanced at the screen on my phone, which I'd set on the ground so we wouldn't be fighting a ghost in the dark, to see if enough time had passed for us to return to the surface. But if I were to believe the clock on my cellphone, no time had passed at all.

"He's stopped time again," I said, more to myself than anyone else, but with Asalluhi manipulating our sense of time, we could've been in that tunnel for three minutes or three days.

I scooped my phone from the ground and made a hasty decision, which was always the best way to make decisions in a life-or-death situation, right? "We know what's waiting for us here. I still think we should go to the next ladder then go back to the surface."

Agnes shrugged. "How's your battery?"

"We should be okay," I answered.

So that's how we ended up walking through a mystery tunnel for an entire day, unsure where we were going or how long we'd been down there or what was going on in the world above us. With the arrival of the locusts, we assumed the boil phase was over, but all of the people who'd been afflicted were most likely still fighting potentially fatal infections. And if they'd been lucky enough to escape the boils, like the child who still clung to Keira as if loosening her grip would lead to a painful death, the fiery hail and locusts would've driven them into whatever shelter they could find.

And that meant there were only two plagues left, two last punishments for an innocent city and thousands of innocent people. Two final attempts to force us to surrender, to convince the world that the Sumerians were not gods to be trifled with.

After walking for what seemed like only an hour or so, we finally came across a ladder, and I offered to check out the world above us and make sure it was relatively safe to go back to the city. I pushed the heavy manhole cover onto the street, but even before climbing out of the tunnel, I could tell something was wrong.

"What is it?" Keira called up to me.

"I have no idea," I said. "Give me a minute."

I hoisted myself onto the street then suddenly realized what was so wrong about my hometown.

It was completely and utterly dark, as if Asalluhi had somehow discovered how to drain all of the light from the world.

The ninth plague, the Three Days of Darkness, had begun.

A STAR IS BORN

(Or my great-grandmother)

It rained for the first time in months the day our daughter was born. A good omen, Arnbjorg claimed. Maybe in Midgard, I'd argued, because the rain was necessary for fertile land, but in Asgard, our crops would grow regardless of the weather. But oddly enough, when Arnbjorg's labor began, she asked me to send for Freyja. And that's when the rain fell in a blinding storm, unusual in its intensity.

As soon as the goddess arrived, I cornered her and demanded to know why she'd cause such weather on a day my wife and I had been eagerly anticipating for months. Freyja looked both angry and hurt by my accusation and tossed her plaited hair over a shoulder. "I'm not the only one in Asgard who can control the weather, Havard."

"Why would Arnbjorg call *you* to her bedside?" I pressed.

Freyja sighed impatiently and pushed past me. "Does it matter? She *has* summoned me, and I imagine she needs my assistance. Wait out here with your brother. I'll send for you when it's over."

Freyja disappeared into the room where my wife labored, and Yngvarr urged me to sit down and reminded me these things could take a while. Why had Arnbjorg called Freyja and not Frigg? And why had she given me no warning that she planned to summon the one goddess I could never trust?

After hours of pacing, the door opened and Freyja waved me inside. My stomach had been in knots the entire time, but the goddess looked pleased and even smiled at me as I hurried past her. And there, sitting up in the bed with a small, swaddled infant pressed to her breast was the reason I lived and died. "We have a daughter," she announced quietly.

I moved the blanket from the baby's face who'd fallen asleep while nursing, but even buried as she was, I could tell she was as breathtakingly beautiful as her mother. "And do you have a name for her?" I asked.

Arnbjorg smiled up at me and answered, "I was thinking Astrid."

Beautiful goddess. A fitting name.

"I think it's perfect," I said. "As is she."

"She is, isn't she?" Arnbjorg whispered. "And Freyja says she's so healthy, Havard. A real blessing."

I took a deep breath and kissed the top of her head, but I *had* to know. "Arnbjorg, why did you want Freyja to help you deliver our child?"

My wife carefully passed our sleeping daughter to me, and I noticed just how drained she was. My cheeks warmed with shame for thinking her choice of midwife was important right now. But my beautiful, kind bride answered me anyway. "Because I trust her, Havard. This rift with Odin is causing divisions across Asgard, and I certainly couldn't call on Frigg. There's no love lost between Freyja and Odin though."

"Perhaps I've judged Freyja too harshly," I admitted.

Arnbjorg smiled and closed her eyes. "Perhaps you have. She has her faults, Havard, but she's loyal. She's given me her word we can rely on her, especially now, and I believe her."

Astrid stirred so I rocked her gently until she slept peacefully again, and when I glanced back toward Arnbjorg, I saw that she'd fallen asleep as well. I cradled my daughter carefully and brought her to meet her uncle. I wasn't at all surprised to find that Badb had arrived and was awaiting an introduction as well. Even though the war goddess had spent quite a bit of time here over the past seven months, we hadn't discussed my prophecy or what I'd asked her to do for my family again. And yet, it always seemed to be there, waiting just beneath the surface in each greeting or farewell and every glance.

Now, she and Yngvarr fussed over Astrid and playfully argued about who would have the honor of holding her first, and since Yngvarr won the argument, I found myself sitting next to Badb as she waited her turn.

"How long has it been since you've had one of your own?" I asked her. I remembered her telling me she'd had several children, but I'd never thought to ask for details.

"A very long time," she said. "It's difficult for a goddess of war to balance raising a child with who she is and how often she's invoked for help among our people. Maybe one day, I won't be needed as often."

I thought there might also be an implication in her hope for more children that she'd found the god with whom she wanted to raise a new family, so I nodded and agreed with her. "One day, I'm sure you'll find time for all your heart desires."

"But for now," she said slyly, "I'm stealing this one from your brother."

And Yngvarr, who didn't want to surrender his niece so soon but could hardly put up a fight without waking the infant he held, had to let Badb win after all.

Several days passed before the war goddess and I found ourselves alone. Yngvarr had gone to Valhalla to extend a personal invitation to our friend and her son, and I was slicing the apples Idun had brought as a gift for my wife. Badb placed a small silver sword on the table in front of me and said, "A gift from the Tuatha Dé for your daughter."

I wasn't sure why she'd waited three days to give it to me with no one around. "Is it also a Sword of Secrets?" I whispered conspiratorially.

Badb laughed and tossed her fiery hair over a shoulder. "Hardly. But I did have it made especially for her. Our smith, Goibniu, crafted it especially for a young girl. I had a feeling about this child. Of course, if I'd been wrong, I had him make a sword for a little boy, too."

I snickered and picked up the sword to admire it. It really was exquisite craftsmanship.

"And does this gift include the lessons from the most feared of the Morrigna?" I asked.

Badb smiled and replied, "Of course. *All* goddesses should be expert swordfighters. And we both know I can't rely on you and Yngvarr to teach her properly."

I laughed again because she *had* actually defeated my brother in mock battle. I'd never been foolish enough to accept her challenge.

Her expression shifted, and she looked around quickly to ensure we were alone. "Have you had any dreams since we last spoke of your prophecy?"

"No," I said. "Nothing different or new anyway. But Arnbjorg told me something recently that I found rather shocking."

Badb lifted an eyebrow in response, so I leaned across the table as if we were conspiring against Asgard itself.

"She's confided in Freyja and told her about our fates," I whispered.

Badb tapped her fingers against the table as she thought about this development. She didn't know Freyja well, but she knew I'd never trusted this goddess, and even now, after she'd proven to be a good midwife for Arnbjorg, I still struggled to accept that Freyja would ever be loyal to anyone but herself. "Well," Badb finally said. "Arnbjorg obviously sees something in this goddess you cannot. Trust your wife's instincts. Mortals tend to have good ones."

"I suppose," I sighed. "And admittedly, my perception of her is colored by my personal standards that aren't entirely fair."

Badb arched an eyebrow at me and asked, "Because she's a woman who takes many lovers? Is that only acceptable for men?"

"No," I corrected. "I don't think it's acceptable for anyone." And then, concerned I may have offended her, I hastily explained, "My parents demonstrated both extremes. My father the constant infidelity, my mother the constant faithfulness. My opinions derive from my own history, and I know—"

"Havard," Badb interrupted. "Your brother has told me all this. I don't fault you for your beliefs, but I do think you should consider Freyja isn't defined by her sexuality or even her love of gold. Discover her other traits, the ones Arnbjorg clearly sees."

Badb was so often like that, insightful and wise and able to help me understand so many things my stubborn brain struggled to grasp. "I'll try. Honestly, I will. I owe my wife that, don't I?"

Badb lifted a shoulder but smiled. She never made me feel foolish when she'd so obviously been right about something.

"Has Yngvarr told you how little time Odin has spent in Asgard lately?" I asked.

"Yes, but it seems fairly normal for him. Your leader doesn't exactly have a great reputation."

"He's not my leader," I mumbled.

Badb snickered and tucked some of her bright red hair

behind an ear. "I think Odin's extended absences from Asgard are a blessing right now. He needs time to get over Áki's presence here, and if the best way for him to do that is by seducing women in Midgard or taking up with a goddess in her own realm, so be it."

"I wish she'd *keep* him in her realm," I said.

"You wish she'd keep whom?" Yngvarr asked, appearing in the doorway with Gunnr and her adopted son. And I couldn't speak so freely in front of a young child, so I answered, "You. But apparently, the Otherworld doesn't want you."

"Why would they?" he joked back. He knew, of course, we hadn't been talking about him and was only playing along.

"Yngvarr," Gunnr said, "would you take Áki to meet your niece?"

"Of course." He held out his hand to escort the child upstairs, and when Áki was out of earshot, she whispered, "With Father so often absent lately, I've heard rumblings of a coup instigated by some of our supporters."

I groaned and ran a hand over my face. This could be dangerous for my family. We didn't have the strength of numbers yet, partly because Odin had all of Valhalla at his disposal. "Do we know who's contemplating usurping Odin's power?" I asked. "We need to intervene. We're not ready."

Gunnr glanced toward Badb, but since Yngvarr and I trusted her, the Valkyrie did, too. "That's the thing. I wouldn't have believed it, but several Valkyries have confirmed it's not just a rumor."

"And the Valkyries have reliable information?" Badb asked, not to insult Gunnr but simply because she was an outsider and didn't know our history.

So Gunnr nodded and explained, "We never report anything unless we've verified it. We've been used as spies for our father since our creation."

"Then who is leading this rebellion against Odin?" I asked.

Gunnr took a deep breath, as if pausing for dramatic effect, and said, "Tyr."

"Tyr?" I repeated. I shook my head as if the motion would dislodge such a ridiculous idea. "He's one of Odin's oldest friends. He'd never betray the All-Father."

Gunnr shrugged as if she'd anticipated my reaction. "That's what I thought, too, but apparently, Tyr thinks Odin's been abusing his power for centuries. Haven't you noticed Odin has been excluding Tyr from more and more decisions? Even the mortals are beginning to forget him."

"What does Yngvarr think about this?" Badb asked.

"He thinks we should approach Tyr, but we need to be careful about it. We don't want word about a conspiracy getting back to Odin before there's an actual conspiracy against him."

I sighed and thought of my three-day-old daughter upstairs. Her birth shouldn't be commemorated with a civil war. But I couldn't abandon my friends either. "All right," I agreed. "We'll talk to Tyr. But we can't risk any harm coming to my child. If we have reason to suspect *anything* isn't quite right, we abandon this ploy."

"We're going to Tyr precisely because we worry about our children's fates," Gunnr said.

She was right, of course. As long as Odin ruled over Asgard, Astrid wouldn't be safe in her own world. And there was nothing I wouldn't do to give my child the future she deserved.

CHAPTER TWELVE

Not only were the sun and moon and stars absent from Baton Rouge, but all of the electric lights had stopped working as well. The darkness that had taken over the city was deep and unforgiving and swallowed the weak beams of flashlights. We'd broken into a bookstore so we could have a place to rest for a while, and I found Agnes and Yngvarr—the two gods I'd been looking for—sitting by the entrance and whispering to one another.

"I don't even want to know what you two are doing," I said, sitting beside them and shining my flashlight at them in feigned accusation.

"Plotting your murder," Agnes said.

I nodded as if I believed her. "Probably deserved, but for what exactly?"

"Latest reason? Shining that damn light in my face."

I set the flashlight on the floor between us and said, "I think Tyr's in danger."

"Gavyn, we've discussed this," Yngvarr replied. "The backup generators at the hospital are—"

"No," I interrupted. "Not because he's on life-support, but

because Odin is with him while there's a citywide blackout. He has the perfect opportunity to disconnect a wire or something and claim the power failure was responsible for Tyr's death."

"Why would he do that?" Yngvarr asked. "Odin's an asshole, but Tyr's one of his closest friends."

I recounted the dream I'd just had, and their faces finally reflected the concern I already felt for our friend. Agnes grabbed my flashlight off the floor and pushed it toward me. "I'm waking everyone up, and we're going to the hospital."

Yngvarr and I waited by the doors, and I was surprised when Keira was the first to join us, considering she still had a three-year-old child physically attached to her. We'd gotten a name out of her, at least, only we weren't exactly sure what she was saying. We'd settled on Sienna, and she hadn't objected, so we were either close enough or she just didn't care what these obnoxious adults called her.

But Keira looked both bewildered and angry, as if trying to wrap her mind around the possibility that Tyr had once led a coup against her father, or maybe that her father would kill him now. And if this coup ever occurred, how would Odin even *remember* Tyr had once led it?

"You know," I said quietly, "the dream ended before I could find out if Tyr ever led any sort of rebellion. He might have changed his mind."

She nodded but seemed as unconvinced as I felt.

The air outside was cold and damp, and Sienna stirred briefly, complaining about the unexpected change in temperature, but we'd found plenty of LSU throw blankets in the bookstore and wrapped two of them around her. She put her head on Keira's shoulder and fell back to sleep as we began the long walk to the hospital.

None of us spoke for the first leg of our journey, but Frey broke our silence by reminding us we were short some of our friends, and they had no idea Tyr might be in more danger than we already feared. "I wish our phones would start working so we could let Thor know what we're doing and why."

"Considering Odin's his father, it's probably better he doesn't know," I argued before remembering Odin was Keira's father, too.

"But Tyr is his best friend," Frey said.

"It's irrelevant," Agnes interjected. "We can't reach him right now anyway."

I pulled my phone out of my pocket, hoping I could finally get a signal just so I could spite her, but the universe—or, more accurately, Asalluhi—was still being a total asshole about the no power, no Wi-Fi, and no cellphone reception thing. Oh, and our clocks and watches still weren't working either. I wasn't sure *why* he had to ensure we didn't know how much time was passing, but he apparently liked to create the illusion that time was meaningless.

We heard the first looters long before we could see them thanks to that whole total darkness thing. Glass shattered and fell against pavement then someone shouted, "Back off!" This was the deep South, where there were more guns than people, and I had a terrible feeling this altercation would end in disaster.

Moments later, my fellow natives proved me right and gunshots joined the chorus of threats. Agnes and I glanced at each other before we both ran toward the looters, hoping those shots were only warnings and we could stop people from collapsing into violent chaos.

At some point, you'd think I'd have learned not to be so naïve.

As we rounded the corner, several guys were ducking beneath the broken glass in the doors to enter the store. Two bodies lay near the shattered glass on the ground, and I aimed my flashlight at them as Agnes crouched by one to check for a pulse. She shook her head and moved to the other body, but I already knew the man was dead. How could he still be alive with so much blood on the ground?

"Your call, Hero," Agnes said. "Keep going or go inside and apprehend them so they can't kill anyone else?"

"First of all, why is it *my* call?" I didn't give her a chance to answer before continuing with my second of all. "And since when do we apprehend people?"

"Since the limited law enforcement in the city can't even receive emergency calls right now," she explained.

"And what would we do with them after apprehending them? You have some dungeon I don't know about?"

"Gavyn," she sighed.

"Seriously, though, you still can't even cross the veil, so even if there's a prison in the Otherworld, we have nowhere to put these guys."

"True," she acknowledged, but she offered nothing else to help me make this impossible decision. So naturally, I flipped her off and told her witches made horrible cops anyway.

"So we're going to the hospital?" she asked.

By now, the rest of the group was catching up to us so I said, "We'll vote. This *is* America, after all."

I couldn't be sure because of how dark it was, but I thought she rolled her eyes at me. But the others were paralyzed with indecision, too, which wasn't helping anyone. I finally got tired of listening to them argue and decided, "Hospital. We owe it to Tyr, so if he's really in danger, we need to help him."

That seemed to be the answer everyone had wanted but had been afraid to say. After all, we were supposed to rescue this world from gods like Asalluhi, and Baton Rouge was under siege because we were here. We all felt the weight of that responsibility, but our friend needed us.

So we left the looters inside the store and the bodies lying near the entrance, even though the city had come alive with gangs breaking windows and setting fires, and trying to start vehicles to steal them only to discover none of them would start. Asalluhi had made sure no one was leaving this city now.

After surviving eight plagues, it really wasn't surprising that those unfortunate people trapped in this city were panicking and that anarchy was descending on us. Worst of all, we had no way of knowing if the Sumerians would attempt the tenth and final plague: the death of firstborn sons. But if they did, they'd likely create their own Passover, giving those left in the city the option to survive if they agreed to serve the gods who'd been tormenting them. And what parents wouldn't agree to anything to save their child?

We resumed our trek to the hospital and given the lawlessness of Baton Rouge's streets, no one paid much attention to the odd group of people walking around with swords and bows and shields. We all agreed to keep an eye out for any more lost children, but otherwise, we'd leave the looters alone. There were too many of them and not enough of us anyway.

I found myself walking next to Keira and offered to carry Sienna for a while, but she shook her head. "It's been a long time since a child has wanted me to carry her. We'll have to give her up soon enough. Let me enjoy it while I can."

"Keira," I said softly, so Agnes wouldn't overhear. "Do you think Áki could have grown up to kill Havard?"

She seemed startled by my question, and her first reaction was to immediately deny her son could have done something like that, but I reminded her Asgard had very different rules of justice. After all, no one had thought twice about the murder of Havard's half-brother or the slaughter of Áki's family.

Keira walked in silence for a while then sighed. "Havard agreed to spare Áki's life. If anything, Áki would've been indebted to him unless something else happened we don't know about yet."

I didn't tell her there was more information Agnes had asked me not to share, but it probably didn't matter anymore. I mean, we'd had to tell them Tyr's life could be in danger because of Odin, so I should've been able to tell Keira everything now. But I didn't. Something held me back, and I feared it was Havard and his annoyingly intrusive curse and overbearing genes.

The hospital loomed in front of us, and we could tell something was wrong before we stepped foot inside. It was too dark, just like the rest of the city.

"Oh, my God," Keira breathed.

"They're just conserving power," Frey said, but the only person he was trying to convince was himself. We all knew better.

We didn't see anyone as we carefully worked our way through the ER, and I thought that was strange considering all of the people who'd been afflicted with boils. It hadn't been *that* long since the infection spread throughout Baton Rouge, so where the hell was everyone? But mostly, I just thought of Tyr and where they'd brought him because this hospital—once the busiest in the city—had been deserted.

As we reached the second floor and emerged from the stairwell into an equally dark hallway, voices finally tiptoed along the otherwise deserted corridors. When they realized they were no longer alone, silence fell all around us like a shroud that would suffocate me if I didn't tear it off. So I called out to the now silent voices, "We're looking for a patient who's in the ICU."

More silence as our lights bobbed along the walls. But

then one familiar voice responded, and my heart dropped into my stomach. "Gavyn?"

Odin. He was still here.

We practically ran over each other as we hurried to the nurses' station, and there, the All-Father and Ull and two staffers sat, their heads bowed and hands clasped in front of them like they'd been praying, but who the hell would Odin and Ull be praying to?

I directed my flashlight at Odin, and his one eye squinted, but I could see it clearly in his face, written so plainly that I didn't need to ask but I heard myself asking anyway. "Tyr?"

Odin's one eye studied the floor again, and he slowly shook his head.

Tyr was dead.

Something happened then, the mood of our group, already bleak, shifted and became oppressive in its hopelessness. For the first time since we rescued her, Keira set Sienna down, who wailed in protest, but Keira slipped into the darkness and vanished.

I sank against a wall and forced myself to ask, "How?"

Agnes scooped Sienna into her arms, and the girl whimpered but didn't fight her. The doctor sighed and rubbed the heel of her hand on her bloodshot eyes. "Generators failed. We had seven patients we couldn't transport when the city was evacuated. None of them made it."

"And Tyr... what... ?" I'd never even thought to ask *why* he was on life support in the first place.

"It's pretty miraculous that Tyr made it out of the labyrinth alive," Ull said, but his voice seemed strange, distant and hollow like he was on autopilot.

"He had water in his lungs," the doctor explained. The tidal wave in the alley... we hadn't walked away unscathed, after all. "The blood loss he suffered made him weaker, and he developed pneumonia. Plus, the toxicology report revealed some unknown poison in his system, most likely from those beetles. It weakened his kidneys and heart. When the respirator quit working, he went into cardiac arrest, and we couldn't—"

"Just stop," I sighed. "Please."

This wasn't how it was supposed to play out. Tyr was a god of war, fated to die in a heroic battle at Ragnarok, a glorious end to a long, courageous life. A warrior's death. But not like this. Not unconscious in a hospital bed because his big, stupid heart stopped working.

Odin abruptly stood up, knocking over his chair, and mumbled, "I need some air."

I grabbed his arm as he passed me, and he jumped and turned on me but didn't have the energy or spirit to fight me. I'd obviously misjudged him, at least about this. I wanted to ask how a god could die when he had his own prophecy, which was supposed to be infallible, but words failed me.

Odin pulled his arm out of my grasp and even though he spoke, I didn't think he was talking to me. "This is my fault. I didn't want any of you going to Sumer, and I should've stopped him. Tyr is dead because of me."

"Odin—" I tried, but he shook his head and lumbered away from me. This time, nobody stopped him.

It hit us then, with all the force of a nuclear strike. This war would demand sacrifices, prices that included our lives, and despite all of the talk about fates and prophecies and destinies, we were each on borrowed time. When Ninurta decided to intervene in the world of men, he'd disrupted the order of both worlds... and no one was safe anymore.

CHAPTER THIRTEEN

By the time the darkness lifted, entire city blocks lay in smoldering ruins and the gravity of our defeat weighed so heavily on us, we seemed incapable of action. We'd failed, and we hadn't really failed at anything before. But we hadn't been able to protect this city, we'd lost Tyr, and we were no closer to finding any of the Sumerian gods than we had been before the plagues hit. Plus, we had the onerous task of having to call Thor and tell him about his friend.

When the ninth plague ended and light returned to Baton Rouge, the veil reopened and Thor and Odin decided they'd bring Tyr home for a traditional funeral. I should've gone, but the twelve-year-old boy within me who would never grow up and get over burying his mother couldn't do it. I made some lame excuse about needing to stay behind and watch over my hometown even though my presence here hadn't done a damn bit of good over the past week.

"Then I'll stay with you," Keira offered. We'd entrusted Sienna into the care of the ICU doctor, which meant we'd most likely never find out if the girl's parents were still alive. We were convinced we'd been right about the girl being part of Asalluhi's plan though. Thor's group had rescued a small boy in a similar situation. They didn't know where his parents were either.

The hits just kept on coming.

"You and Tyr had been friends longer than I can even imagine," I said. "You need to go."

"I'm not leaving you here alone," she insisted.

Agnes sat beside me and stared absently out the window for a few seconds before offering, "I'll stay. As much as I hate to admit it, Gavyn's right. You need to be there, Keira."

I had to say it, the one thing we'd *all* been dancing around but couldn't bear to verbalize, but Thor and Odin had already returned to Asgard and we were running out of time. "It won't matter, Keira. If a Sumerian Passover occurs, we can't do a goddamn thing to stop it, so it won't matter if we're all here or not."

"We can offer our lives instead," she said, which was exactly what I'd expected her to say.

"No, but I can offer *mine*. I'm somehow tied into the outcome of this war. It's been my life they've wanted all along. If Ninurta is resorting to murdering children, we can't possibly win anyway."

Keira wouldn't meet my gaze. She knew I was right.

"Go home," I told her. "Tyr deserves the most grandiose send-off Asgard has ever seen."

Keira bit her lip and nodded, fighting back tears that I wanted to cry with her, but instead, my heart felt numb. Agnes and I returned our attention to the window overlooking my city. I have no idea how long we sat like that, just silently staring at the plumes of smoke against the pale blue sky. I was so immersed in my self-pity, I didn't even notice Ra had joined us, so when he spoke, he scared the shit out of me, and I may or may not have jumped a little at the unexpected sound of his voice.

"I couldn't find the sun," he said.

Agnes and I slowly turned toward him, blinking stupidly at the annoyingly handsome god who'd apparently shown up to confuse the hell out of us. "It's right there," I said carefully, pointing to the midday sun in the sky... exactly where it belonged.

But Ra shook his head. "No, over the last three days. I kept trying to bring it back, but I couldn't *find* it. How can a god like Asalluhi be more powerful than me?"

I really wasn't in the mood to soothe wounded egos, so I waved him off and decided to ignore him. But Baba Yaga apparently couldn't leave it alone. "Our power is shifting all the time. You might have been one of the strongest gods in all the worlds at one time, but when we retreated into our own realms, we became like athletes who stopped training. The talent may still be there, but our bodies can no longer handle the exertion."

"Badb—" he started, but I couldn't ignore *this*.

"Agnes," I corrected.

Ra sighed and tried again. "Agnes, if you're right, if we're all so out of shape now, how can we possibly save this planet?"

"*We* can't," she said. "That's why we have the heroes."

I snorted and she shot me a look that dared me to challenge her, so I accepted. "In case you haven't noticed, we heroes are as useless as you gods."

"You're letting this one setback reorient your entire outlook on this battle. You nearly killed Ninurta once. With his own spear, no less. How can you believe you're so impotent now?"

"Hey," I snapped. "Nobody *ever* said I'm impotent. Take that back."

Agnes narrowed her eyes at me as if trying to decide if I were really this stupid. She must've decided I was because she snapped back, "I'm obviously talking about how much power you have, not your—"

"Don't say it," I interrupted. "You're not allowed to talk about it or it may never work again. You probably *would* curse me and make me impotent."

"I honestly can't remember why I thought it would be a good idea to come in here," Ra said.

"You were obviously desperate," I agreed.

Ra nodded, and Agnes tried to change the subject, but I couldn't forgive her just yet for questioning my *potency*.

"Where's Anubis?" she asked.

"Trying to determine if Anhur is still alive."

"How?" I asked, interested in something Ra had to say for the first time since... well, since forever.

"By communing with the dead," Ra explained. "Specifically, the Egyptian heroes who've been assisting the gods like my son."

"Your son," I repeated flatly. More family drama. I mean, seriously, what the hell was *wrong* with these godly kids? Was this all like some middle child syndrome?

"Anhur," Ra said. "You didn't know he's my son?"

I waved a hand in his direction and lied. "Of course I knew that."

Agnes snickered while I silently told Havard he was an asshole for not providing me with relevant information for once. He'd throw completely useless trivia at me like Baba Yaga but not vitally important relationships of the gods we were fighting and allying ourselves with? And Havard was keeping whatever else he knew about the Egyptian gods to himself, forcing me to ask, "So your demigods get to team up with the bad guys and still go to the Egyptian Valhalla?" I mean, what kind of crackpot system was this?

"There is no Egyptian Valhalla," Ra replied a little defensively.

"Besides," Agnes added, "Anhur most likely is alive. We haven't fought him since the lion army attack."

Ra nodded and grabbed the notepad and pen from the hotel's desk. "Which means we still have to find him, Asalluhi, Inanna, Medeina, Nergal, Ninurta, Paricia, and Zababa."

I crossed my arms and narrowed my eyes at him. "You listed those gods in alphabetical order... like you already *had* a list of them handy and just wanted to make sure we all remembered who we were fighting."

So Ra handed me the list and shrugged. "Seemed convenient and like a good time for us to itemize who was still alive and who we'd eventually have to fight."

"I want a copy of that," Agnes told me, so I handed *her* the list and told her I'd just lose it anyway.

Admittedly, Ra's presence and the ensuing bickering, most of which was good-natured except for the whole impotency thing, had at least taken my mind off Tyr's death and why all of our friends weren't with us. Around lunchtime, Ra crossed the veil and returned with bowls of the most vile looking crap ever *put* in a bowl, but he gave me one anyway. Agnes handed me one of those little bottles of vodka you'd get from a hotel's mini-bar or on an airplane or something, and I wanted to ask her where the hell she'd even *gotten* it since this hotel didn't *have* mini-bars, but I decided I'd rather drink it than accuse her, once again, of being a witch with the admittedly superb ability to make alcoholic beverages magically appear.

"Mulukhiya," Ra announced, as if that would make me want to eat what he'd given me. I took a long swig from the vodka then thought, "*What the hell. I'm going to die soon anyway*," and dipped the flat bread into the slimy soup. I gagged before the bread reached my lips and decided I needed more vodka.

"Here," Ra laughed as he tried to take the bowl from me,

but the vodka was kicking in so I held out a hand and stopped him. This slime stew was going down.

I dipped the flat bread into the dark green, mucusy soup again and held my breath, but go figure: it tasted exactly like you'd expect dark green, mucusy soup to taste.

I rushed to the bathroom to spit it out... or vomit, whichever came first... and Agnes laughed at me then said the unforgivable. "Bet Hunter could've kept it down."

I stood in the doorway to the bathroom and glared at her. "Take that back."

She just shrugged and smiled mischievously at me. "He has a much more adventurous palate, and apparently, a much stronger stomach."

"That's it. Take me to the Otherworld right now with this... mucus stew."

"Can't," she said far too happily. "We need to guard this city, remember?"

I squinted at her and returned to my seat, but if she thought I was going to let this challenge go, she didn't know me nearly as well as she thought she did. Sure, I'd probably be dead by the time I had the chance to enter into a gross-out contest with my best friend, but we could totally do it from Valhalla. And maybe being dead would give me an advantage since I wouldn't have to worry about Ra's mucus stew killing me.

I finished the flat bread and vodka but pretended like the Hero Poison Ra had tried to kill me with didn't exist, and I may have even dozed off for a while because the next time I glanced at the sky, it had turned to those familiar shades of pink and orange indicating sunset. Agnes and Ra were watching the sky's transformation, and she somehow knew I was awake or at least sober again. "If they're going to imitate the tenth plague, it'll begin soon," she said without turning around to look at me.

"That's what the vodka was for," I guessed. "A farewell present?"

"No, that was for the mulukhiya."

"And there haven't been any announcements?" I asked. "No chances to spare lives in exchange for obedience and servitude?"

Agnes shook her head. "Nothing. Radio silence all day."

"You know," Ra said, "your surrender won't stop anything. It might save a few lives now, but how many will it cost in the long run?"

"What are we supposed to do?" I snapped. "Sit here and drink while people die?"

"Of course not," he answered. "We can't even find Asalluhi on our own—we learned that the hard way. But with the veil reopened, I suggest we fight magic with magic."

"Isis," Agnes said. "She only helped us before because she got something out of it. What can we possibly offer her now?"

"Well," Ra said a little *too* nonchalantly, which should have alerted me that he was going to be a smartass at my expense but maybe I wasn't as sober as I thought. "Gavyn's insisting he's rather *potent*, so—"

"Dude, I don't care if you're an ally. I *will* kick your ass," I warned before realizing he was just messing with me.

"Any ideas aside from pimping out Gavyn?" Agnes asked, but she looked a little too amused by the thought of turning me into a gigolo.

"Yeah," Ra said. "I have another idea. She'll want the same thing she's always wanted: more power. She has no interest in this world anymore, so I'll offer her a higher seat in ours."

"Is that literal?" I asked, just to be a pain in the ass for the whole prostitution thing. "Like... a taller bar stool or something?"

But Ra didn't skip a beat, which actually went a long way

in making me like the guy. "Yes, we intend to raise every chair and stool in her house by six inches."

"Only six inches, huh?" I shot back.

"Gavyn," Agnes sighed, but Ra shrugged and said, "She has a lot of American made furniture, so yeah, that's as high as they'll go."

And since the bastard had stumped me, I just stood there for a few minutes waiting for someone to say *something*, but they were apparently sadists who enjoyed watching me squirm. Finally, Agnes nodded toward the window and said, "Sun's almost down. Go get Isis."

As soon as Ra crossed the veil, I shot Agnes my best "You're a traitor" scowl, which only seemed to please her. I was mid-question about how long this would take when Ra returned with the same beautiful but dour goddess who sighed heavily and glowered at the Baton Rouge skyline. "What now?" she demanded.

"We need your help to find Asalluhi. If we don't kill him soon, a curse may fall on this city that kills every first born son," Ra explained.

"Whoa," I exclaimed. "*I'm* a first born son."

"Just now figuring that out, huh?" Agnes retorted.

Isis looked me over quickly then turned back to Ra. "Explain to me again how *this* guy," she even paused to jerk a thumb in my direction, "is supposed to save the world."

"We're thinking it has something to do with being the last guy Ninurta and his crew would expect," Agnes answered, although everyone knew it wasn't a truthful answer. Ninurta had known about me all along.

But Isis nodded anyway like Agnes's explanation made perfect sense, so I pouted a little harder until the Egyptian goddess sighed again and motioned toward the door. "All right. This one's a freebie since even I draw the line at murdering children. Plus, I always hated Asalluhi."

"Thank you, Isis," Ra said.

She held up a finger and cut off anything else he was going to say. "But this is it. I didn't want to make enemies of gods I may have once considered friends. Inanna and I have a long history together, and I won't fight her."

"That's completely fair," Ra agreed.

Personally, I didn't think it was so fair considering Inanna had shown up in *my* world and started blowing shit up and killing people, but no one seemed interested in my opinion. Of course, no one had been interested in my opinion since this whole thing began, so you'd think I'd have been used to that by now.

I was still sulking a bit as I followed the gods outside where the air was quickly cooling in that late fall in the South kind of way. I shivered and zipped up my jacket as Isis closed her eyes and whispered, "Don't move."

We immediately complied and froze in place, waiting for her to explain why we were just standing in the hotel's parking lot. But then I noticed the asphalt shimmering like a mirage, only I knew it wasn't. This hotel had been here for years, so it wasn't part of Asalluhi's deceptions, yet he'd clearly planned on *something* transforming as soon as we stepped foot outside. The world around us was attempting to change, to transform the familiar into the strange, like circular streets that would always bring us back to where we'd started. Or like an alleyway filled with water that could kill a god.

Isis was obviously fighting the spell, undoing its attempted illusions and deceptions, and the rippling asphalt stilled. She opened her eyes and spoke over her shoulder. "Stay close behind me. I can lead you to him, but he has curses all over this city."

"Can you sense one that reenacts the vengeful spirit that passed through Egypt taking lives?" Ra asked.

We were *all* getting nervous about how quickly the sun seemed to be setting. It was an inescapable reminder that we were running out of time.

"No," Isis said. "I'm afraid it doesn't work that way. But I'm confident I can get you to him." She waved a hand at us, indicating we should follow her, so we obeyed but watched the buildings and streets warily, expecting them to transform into a nightmarish labyrinth at any moment.

Occasionally, Isis would slow down and murmur an incantation, so we'd slow down, too, waiting silently as she broke the spell so we could stay in the Baton Rouge I knew rather than the Baton Rouge Asalluhi wanted to create. I was so focused on following Isis that I wasn't even paying attention to where we were going. By the time I realized we'd ventured into my dad's neighborhood, twilight had given way to the heavy darkness of night, and we were all on edge, wondering if I'd just drop dead or if something—or, more accurately, a lot of somethings—would swoop down and fight me first.

But being in my father's neighborhood only made me think I really had no reason to trust this goddess who claimed she was helping us yet admitted she was Inanna's friend. Leading us here may have been Asalluhi's greatest trick.

Isis stopped in the middle of the street and inhaled a sharp, quick breath. "He knows we're here. Look." She pointed to the same front yard where I once hunted huge salamanders with Mike Hebert, the asthmatic kid who lived a few houses down. When we found one, we'd stick it in a glass jar and poke holes in the lid so it wouldn't suffocate, and we lined them up on my porch, convinced we'd have an entire army of salamanders at our disposal.

And really, the only good a salamander army would do *anyone* was to scare the girls in the second grade with us, and that's exactly what we intended to do. But my mom walked onto the porch, saw the glass jars with the serpentine salamanders inside, screamed, and yelled at us to set them all free... far away from the house.

I wasn't at all sure why *that* memory, of the thousands of memories I had of my childhood home, resurfaced at that moment. As I stared at my dad's yard, thinking about Mike Hebert and all those salamanders who'd been enjoying the soggy ground after three straight days of rain, I didn't even notice that the blades of grass sprouted legs and began to crawl over each other. And while they didn't resemble salamanders at all, I still couldn't shake that memory.

Agnes wrinkled her nose and bumped into me as she backed away from the yard. "Praying mantises," she hissed.

Ra glanced at Isis and asked, "Can you turn them back into grass?"

"I'm trying. But I think you need to draw him outside."

I snorted and both Agnes and Ra shot me a strange look, so I just shrugged. "Why the hell would he come out here? He's outnumbered, and it's a lot easier to defend himself inside the house, don't you think?"

"We'd need something he wants," Agnes agreed. Her eyes widened for a second then she smiled and added, "Like the Sword of Prophecy."

"Um... sure, I'd like that, too," I said.

Agnes shook her head and grabbed my arm. "Go to Odin's palace and get the replica. Keira can get you back here. Hurry."

I had so many reasons to argue with her, so many excuses for why this was a stupid idea and it would never work, but when I opened my mouth to begin reciting that very long list, she was no longer beside me. Instead, the massive wall of Asgard stood before me, and a gate swung open with a mystified Heimdall gawking at me. "Gavyn? How did you get here?"

I folded my arms, pissed off that not only had I been

abducted and dragged all over Earth, but I was apparently being transported to different worlds against my will now, too. "Agnes sent me."

"Agnes," he repeated flatly.

I grunted but refused to call her anything else, mostly because I was still pissed about her sending me to Asgard in the first place. "Yeah, the Irish war goddess who goes around pretending to be the world's first witch even though she's *really* a super hot redhead."

"Why did Badb—"

"Agnes," I interrupted.

Heimdall sighed and waved me inside the walls. "How did *Agnes* get you here?"

"How the hell should I know? I guess she just opened the veil and pushed me through."

"Why?" Heimdall seemed to think about it because he shook his head and quickly added, "Never mind. I think I know why."

"As much as I'd love to stick around and engage in this pointless discussion, I'm kinda in the middle of a magical supernatural wizarding battle."

"I don't think wizarding is a word," Heimdall pointed out.

"Who are you? Merriam-Webster?"

"That company is actually named after several people," he continued to annoyingly point out.

"Why do you know that?" I snapped.

"Why *don't* you know that?" he retorted.

In the distance, pinpoints of light arched through the sky, diverting my attention from my argument with the Norse gatekeeper.

"They've set arrows ablaze and are shooting them over Tyr's body as he's set out to sea," Heimdall explained.

"Oh," I whispered. What else could I say? Part of me, a *big* part of me, had been hoping the entire funeral was over and I wouldn't have to witness it. I already held onto too many painful memories of final goodbyes. But as I watched the arrows escort Tyr to his final home, I had the sinking feeling it wouldn't be the last goodbye I'd have to make.

I cleared my throat and turned back to Heimdall. "Why aren't you over there with your family?"

"Who would watch the gate? Besides, I can see from here."

"Heimdall, I have to get something from Odin's palace. We need it in order to defeat Asalluhi. Can you send me back to Agnes once I return?"

He nodded and didn't even ask me what I was about to steal from Odin. Perhaps he just assumed Odin would have given it to me anyway, or perhaps his mind was still on the shore with the others saying goodbye to one of the kindest and bravest gods I'd ever know.

I ran to Odin's palace where one of his servants allowed me inside but followed me to the sword room. He kept asking me if I needed assistance, or if he should call for his master, but I ignored him and resisted the temptation to break the glass case, just for the hell of it.

"Gavyn, if you'd just let me—" he started, but I cut him off by holding up the sword and snapping, "Do you really think it's a good idea to annoy the hell out of a guy holding a sword?"

He looked more surprised than worried, but at least he shut up and I ran back to the gate where Heimdall was waiting. His attention was still fixed on the ceremony far from us where only his eyes could see, and while he kept his attention there, he put a hand on my shoulder and said, "Be careful, Gavyn. I'm in no hurry to witness more of these."

And just like that, I was back in Baton Rouge, standing beside Agnes as if I'd never left, only holding the sword that so closely resembled Havard's, the sword both sides of this war wanted badly enough to commit foolish mistakes.

"Isis," Agnes whispered, "put some kind of spell on this sword to make it glow. If it were the real Sword of Light, it would be glowing in Gavyn's hands."

Isis complied, and the sword emitted a faint glow. I may have audibly gasped seeing a sword that *looked* so much like the one I coveted, but even if I hadn't just stolen the replica, I would've known this wasn't the real Sword of Prophecy. It was just in me, this sword and its power and Havard's attachment, and I knew when I found the real sword, it would feel like an extension of myself, just as Havard had always felt it was an extension of him.

But Asalluhi wasn't privy to those memories or the knowledge Havard's genes held, and as we approached my father's house, the door opened and a man stepped onto the porch, his eyes all fire and envy. Isis scoffed and tossed her sleek, black hair over a shoulder, lifting her chin slightly as if defying the god whose magic was greater than her own. "Asalluhi."

And the Sumerian god of magic slowly smiled at me and said, "Gavyn... I think we each have something the other wants."

CHAPTER FOURTEEN

Something that *I* wanted? I somehow doubted he was offering to pack up and go home in exchange for the sword, so I shrugged and said, "When I was fifteen, I wanted Winona Ryder—the one from *Beetlejuice*. You got her in there?"

Ra shot me a confused glance and asked, "Why? She was so weird and morbid."

"But hot."

"There are lots of hot girls that aren't obsessed with death."

"Would you both shut up?" Isis scolded.

"Sorry," we both mumbled.

Asalluhi's attention had never left the sword in my hands, and I was getting worried he'd soon discover it was a fake. But all the spells in the world couldn't give it the kind of power my real sword contained. We needed to get him away from the door in case he had his own battalion behind him, and I had to assume the guy wasn't stupid, so why would he confront us alone?

"Okay, I give up. What do you have that you think I want?" I asked.

"In the future," Agnes whispered, "you might not want to preface anything you say with 'I give up.'"

"Point taken," I whispered back.

Asalluhi yelled into the house, and feet shuffled as another figure appeared in the doorway, dragging someone behind him, only not just *any* someone.

"Keira," I gasped. Not my Valkyrie, but my original Keira, my ex-girlfriend whom I'd been in love with for almost three years and at one point, had considered marrying. We'd broken up over a year ago, and I hadn't even seen her in six months, so how the hell did these assholes know about her? How long had they been watching me?

Just thinking about it made me sick and nauseated. I swallowed even though my mouth was suddenly dry and forced my feet to stay still. I could sense that uncontrollable anger trying to take over, those genes of my ancestor attempting a rescue that would likely only result in her death. So I took a deep breath and asked her, "Are you all right?"

"*What a stupid question,*" I thought. "*Of course she's not all right. She's been kidnapped and held for ransom and just learned* you're *the dumbass who's supposed to save her.*"

But Keira nodded and actually looked relieved to see me. Confused, but relieved.

"What do you want?" I asked Asalluhi.

He nodded toward the sword in my hand and asked, "Where'd you find it?"

"What difference does it make?" I snapped.

"Because I'm asking, and right now, you're the only one with something to lose."

"Actually," I bluffed, "now that I have the Sword of Light, it would be ridiculously easy to kill you."

"If it were so easy, you'd have killed me already," he said.

And if it were the real Sword, I wouldn't part with it so willingly, so I just stood there, vacillating between charging the porch in a stupid and desperate attempt to free my ex-girlfriend and end the curse on Baton Rouge, and wishing Agnes would *do* something because she was way smarter than me and I was clearly out of my element here.

"So," Asalluhi said, "where did you find the sword?"

"Asgard," I answered.

He sighed as if he'd already known the Sword of Prophecy was in Asgard and demanded, "*Where* in Asgard?"

I remembered the list of names Ninurta had shown me. Somehow, the Sumerians knew a lot more about the real sword's fate than my Norse and Irish allies. Of course, if someone among the Norse really had been conspiring with the Sumerians, Asalluhi could easily know more than me about the sword's hiding place. Regardless, I decided the more lies I piled on, the more likely it would be that he'd discover we were really making this all up. So I eyed him suspiciously but told him the truth about where I'd found this sword. "It was in Odin's palace."

"Odin?" Asalluhi repeated. He sounded completely baffled, and I didn't really know what to make of that.

"Yeah, he didn't know there was anything special about it, but I knew what I was looking for."

Asalluhi crossed his arms and asked, "And how did he get it?"

"He doesn't remember," I answered truthfully.

Asalluhi narrowed his eyes and stared at me for so long, I actually got a little uncomfortable. "I don't believe you," he finally said. "You've been stalling, and I don't appreciate how much of my time you've wasted."

Given he was calling our bluff, the *smart* thing to do would've been begging or negotiating, but we all know by now that's not my MO. I relaxed my hold on those godly genes, or that far more violent person inside me, and practically flew onto the porch, even though the lawn was still crawling with praying mantises. The god of magic was caught off guard, but not so much that I had any significant advantage. I had no idea where the sword he suddenly held came from, but he deflected my attack while Keira was dragged back inside the house.

Isis dropped to the ground, digging her fingers into the dirt while those slender green bugs crawled up her arms. I shuddered—how could anyone *not* be grossed out by all these insects *crawling on people?*—but advanced on Asalluhi again. Maybe I could at least distract him long enough for my allies to start pulling their weight. Asalluhi parried and knocked me back against the porch railing, and I had a brief sensation of déjà vu. It had only been a week or so since the last time I'd stood on my dad's porch fighting for my life.

From inside the house, Keira screamed my name, and my pulse quickened and my legs threatened to give out on me. I couldn't reach her. Asalluhi blocked the door, and God knew what they were doing to her. And I couldn't save her. Keira was going to die because she'd been unlucky enough to fall in love with me, a relationship that apparently could curse a person for life.

A praying mantis landed on Asalluhi's face, surprising us both. He flinched and swatted it away, only for another one to take its place. By the time I figured out Isis had cast her own spell and was now controlling the insects, Asalluhi's face was swarming in a blur of wings and spindly legs.

I ran the fake Sword of Prophecy through the Sumerian god's heart and tried to look all cool and badass by pulling it out and charging inside, but the damn thing was stuck.

I'm still not sure how something like that even happens. I mean, it went *into* his chest easily enough, so why the hell wouldn't it come *out* just as easily?

Anyway, Agnes thrust a different sword at me and yelled, "Go find her!" Several demigods had appeared out of nowhere —or the backyard but claiming they just miraculously appeared out of nowhere makes a better story—so Ra and Agnes were preoccupied, leaving me alone to rescue my ex-girlfriend.

I darted inside the house where I'd grown up, wondering if I'd ever be able to come back here... you know, if I weren't fated to die and all that. But given how many gods, heroes, and giants had tried to kill me here, I figured I was pretty much scarred by this place now.

Two demigods guarded a closed door, my old bedroom, and I figured out they were heroes and not gods because the bastards drew handguns as soon as they saw me and gods had that whole superiority complex when it came to guns. I raised my shield, and the bullets ricocheted off its magical barrier and splintered the paneling on the wall.

Naturally, my eternally dumb ass hadn't brought any weapon invented in the last millennium, so I was stuck behind my shield while the other two dumbasses kept firing at me and demolishing my dad's wall.

A sliver of light broke across the dark ceiling, and the bullets pelting my shield stopped. Shouting in a language I didn't speak replaced the sound of firearms discharging, but the light disappeared just as quickly as it had disrupted their attack. Only I was pretty sure I heard the clicking of a door closing as the light vanished.

Keira.

I risked lowering my shield to peek around it, half expecting the ceasefire to be some ploy to... oh, I don't know, *lower my shield so they could blow my head off*. But one of the heroes lay on the floor, hands clasped tightly over his bloody thigh. The knife he'd been stabbed with had been tossed onto the floor beside him. The other hero tried opening the door, but Keira must've pushed something in front of it, most likely the dresser my dad used for storing all of my mom's old clothes because he'd never been able to part with them.

The uninjured demigod kicked the door, but if Keira *had* somehow managed to move the dresser in front of it, that door wasn't budging. I puzzled over how she'd managed to move it so quietly and quickly for a few seconds before realizing two things: One, I was wasting precious time since both demigods were distracted, and two, I'd come here with a goddess of magic. Thinking anyone or anything should follow natural laws of physics only reinforced my immeasurable stupidity.

Now that I'd decided to stop standing around pondering the many wonders of supernatural science, I really needed to kill the assholes trying to kill Keira and me. And even though I'd never held anyone hostage, it seemed they should've killed her already, like as soon as Asalluhi had a sword run through his heart. But what did I know about kidnapping people?

In one of my many immeasurably brilliant moments, I lowered my shield and attacked the guy still trying to kick down the door. Clearly, this guy was my competition for dethroning me as the World's Biggest Idiot. The injured demigod tried to rise, so I sliced my sword toward the general vicinity of his neck while flipping my shield and hitting the Pretender to the Throne over the head with it.

Yeah, really. But give me a break; I'd only been at this hero business for a month.

Not surprisingly, my arch-rival blinked and backed away from me, looking more puzzled than hurt, but his slow attempt to figure out what the hell was going on gave me a few seconds to follow up the head-bonking with a head-separation. And while I was feeling rather heroic and deserving of my other title as Savior of the World, I heard the other demigod, whom I apparently *hadn't* killed in my run-by, groaning but grabbing something metallic off the hardwood floor.

Something like a knife that I'd stupidly left by the guy who'd been trying to kill me since I stepped into this hallway.

I felt the knife pierce my back before I could turn around and block it with my shield. A body thumped against the wall, and Agnes was suddenly beside me, examining the wound as she tried to decide if it would be more dangerous to leave the knife where it was or remove it. Ra shouted to Isis, something about all of the threats being neutralized or maybe less clichéd and corny phrases, but come on: I had a knife in my back and wasn't paying particularly close attention to what people were saying.

But thinking about my injury made me snicker and I told Agnes, "I have an actual list of people I expect to stab me in the back. That guy wasn't on it."

"I need to get you to a doctor," she said.

"There aren't any doctors here," I pointed out.

The door opened and Keira stood hesitantly in the doorway. Who could blame her for not trusting these gods after everything she'd just survived? Isis hovered close behind her, protective and suspicious. The goddess must've decided Keira's life was her responsibility, and she had no intention of failing. I kinda liked that about Isis, this aloofness coupled with an inexhaustible determination.

Keira's attention finally fell on me, and she took a step toward me but Isis put an arm around her and said, "I'm going to get you out of this city now."

"Gavyn," Keira whispered.

"You can trust her." I took a deep breath and added, "I'm so sorry this happened to you."

Keira's expression shifted, but Agnes grabbed my arm and announced, "We have to go now. They'll take care of her, Gavyn. Don't worry."

"Wait," Keira begged. "Will he...?"

Agnes offered her a sympathetic smile and promised, "I'm taking him to the person I trust most for this sort of thing. And Isis will bring you somewhere safe, where no one can find you and hold you hostage again. That's also a promise."

And in that moment, I had a feeling I'd never see her again. Sure, I wasn't in the habit of hanging out with my exes, but she lived in Baton Rouge. The possibility of running into each other was always there, and it just hit me that my life as I'd always known it was over. My friends, my job, my apartment, my exes and the women I'd once planned on becoming my exes... it was all gone now.

Agnes put her arm around me, but before she could whisk me away to this doctor of hers, I shot Keira one last glance and said, "I'm sorry, you know."

"For what?" she whispered.

"For not taking you to the Basilica in St. Louis when we were there. You wanted to go, and I wanted to sleep in and we ran out of time and you never got to see it. I should've taken you."

"Oh, Gavyn," she sighed.

But I never had the chance to hear if she forgave me or not, or even to ask Agnes where we were going. Of course, that question was soon answered anyway when my father's house and all of Baton Rouge, all of *Earth* disappeared when Agnes crossed the veil. But we hadn't traveled to Asgard.

Badb, the most feared war goddess in all the realms, had brought me to the Otherworld.

CHAPTER FIFTEEN

Agnes sighed and cursed under her breath, so naturally, I assumed that was the proper Tuatha Dé greeting and sighed and cursed when some guy walked past us.

"Gavyn," Agnes groaned. "Can you not be yourself for a little while?"

"Depends."

She arched an eyebrow at me and prodded, "On?"

"On whom you want me to be."

"Someone incapable of speaking."

"In that case, no. And honestly, I'm surprised you'd even ask."

"Crossing the veil isn't precise," she explained, wisely choosing to ignore anything I had to say about my inability not to annoy the hell out of her. "I need to get you to our healer, Dian Cécht, but we're not terribly close."

"Dian? She sounds hot."

"*He* is. And I'll let him know you think so, too."

I cringed but considering I still had a knife sticking out of my back, it was just as much from pain as it was Agnes's threat to tell some guy I was totally into him. A voice in the distance called her name, and I thought I recognized that voice, but my vision was blurring and my feet stumbled over each other. Agnes kept me from falling, but the grass looked incredibly soft and the sunshine was warm, like a blanket fresh from the dryer, and I *wanted* to fall and just sleep for a few thousand years.

Instead, the guy who'd called her name jogged toward us, and my fuzzy vision combined with my fuzzy thoughts took a while to match his face with a name. "Cadros?" I said. "I was wondering where you'd disappeared to."

Cadros responded, but I didn't quite hear him or if I did, my rapidly deteriorating grasp on consciousness slipped right at that moment because I have no idea what he said to me or how I got to the house I woke up in. But when I next opened my eyes, lying on my stomach in a comfortable bed within a room filled with sunlight from the open windows, I smiled to myself and had a brief moment of believing the past month had all been a nightmare.

"Hunter," I mumbled into my pillow. "You won't believe the dream I had. How drunk were we?"

"When?" he asked.

"Recently." The room spun a bit so I closed my eyes and added, "*Very* recently. I think I'm still drunk."

"More like drugged," he said.

"We don't do drugs."

"It's just their version of morphine. It'll wear off."

I forced my eyes open again and managed to get his face into focus as I realized nothing in this room looked familiar. I had no idea where I was, which wasn't necessarily unheard of with Hunter and me, but he'd been sitting by my bed reading, as if waiting for me to wake up. And as much as I didn't want to, I took a shaky breath and asked, "Otherworld?"

He nodded and put his book on the nightstand. "Yeah." Hunter ran his fingers through his hair and took his own shaky breath. "Gavyn, I wish... I don't know, I just wish I could help somehow. What you're going through, saving the world and all that, and here I am—"

"The Sumerians kidnapped Keira," I interrupted.

Hunter nodded again. "I know."

"How did they know about her? How much do they know about *me*?"

"Probably better not to ask."

I grunted at him and slowly sat up, which prompted Hunter to jump from his seat and help me like I'd suddenly become some ninety-year-old invalid. Of course, I *felt* like a ninety-year-old invalid, but it's not like I'd ever admit that. But then I remembered I'd been completely convinced I'd never see my best friend again, and I kinda wanted to hug him but I also didn't want him to make it a thing and question my sexuality yet again so I just said, "What've you been up to while I've been out there getting my ass kicked?"

"I've been here *not* getting my ass kicked."

I narrowed my eyes at him and said, "That's about to change."

Hunter snickered then lowered his gaze like he always did when he was about to say something difficult. I had a terrible suspicion what he was struggling to say and I didn't want to talk about it either, but the bastard went and started it anyway. "I heard about Tyr."

I cleared my throat thinking of all the words I *wanted* to say but the only one that came out was, "Yeah."

"Dude, *gods* are out there dying."

What he'd *meant* to say was more like, "If gods are getting killed in this war, what chance do you have?"

And what I would've responded with would've been something like, "None. I already told you I'm going to die. You just refused to believe it."

But instead I just nodded because he hadn't said what he

really wanted to, and I still didn't have the heart to shatter his illusion that I could walk away from this struggle and go back to a now broken Baton Rouge and we could just pick up our lives exactly as they'd been when we left and everything would eventually be okay.

"And our city," I added, my voice tripping a bit as I thought about how damaged it had been simply because it had been my home.

"My dad..." Hunter's voice tripped, too, so I finished for him.

"Pretty sure he got out in time," I assured him.

"Cell service is jammed," he said. "Calls to Baton Rouge numbers aren't going through."

"Not surprised." Then, to change the subject since I couldn't stand seeing Hunter sad and worried and knowing he was utterly alone here, I pointed to one of the windows and suggested he show me around and fill me in on what he'd been doing.

"More like *who*," he said.

"This is *so* unfair," I complained.

He led me outside where a group of gods and goddesses scattered nervously, trying to pretend like they *hadn't* been standing around spying on us. Just to mess with them, I shouted, "I'm telling Agnes!" after their retreating backs before thinking, "*No one here knows who that is, dumbass.*" So I told that voice to cut me some slack—I'd been pumped up with Otherworldly morphine and was still a little high, but that voice just told me being completely sober wouldn't change the fact that I'm still a dumbass.

"Gavyn," Hunter sighed. "Did you hear *anything* I just said?"

"Totally," I lied, and of course, he knew I was lying.

"Remember the Ole Miss game?" he asked.

I shrugged. There had been a lot of football games over

the years, and honestly, I didn't remember most of them. Beer may or may not have been the culprit into the loss of those memories.

"The one we were watching when the Sumerians first showed up," he said. "The one that got interrupted not only by the news but the goddesses who kidnapped us."

"Keira isn't a goddess. She's a Valkyrie."

He waved me off as if that were completely inconsequential. But I was actually curious where his line of thinking was going, so I dropped the whole goddess versus Valkyrie thing and said, "Yeah, of course I remember it."

"I never had the chance to tell you what you'd have to do if I won."

I laughed because it seemed so absurd to finish our bet now. We'd eventually found out the score, and Hunter had won the bet, so I crossed my arms and said, "And what's it going to be? Something worse than repeatedly getting stabbed and mauled, fighting gods and flaming zombie monkeys—"

"Flaming *what?*"

"—and constantly facing my impending death? Whatever you've got, *Julian*... bring it on."

He pointed a finger at me and said, "We're coming back to the flaming zombie monkeys. But since I won, you're drinking a Crimson Horton. *The whole thing.*"

I must've visibly paled. I *felt* like I was visibly paling and maybe even doing some preemptive vomiting. I'd never squelched on one of our bets before, but my mind raced with ways to get me out of this, and I seriously considered shouting for Agnes and claiming I was too sick to be moving around and needed a few weeks to convalesce.

"I can't," I lied. "Don't you know football season has been canceled?"

Hunter waved me off. "Doesn't matter. I'll settle for your debt being paid back right here in Murias—"

"In where?" I interrupted, somehow knowing already exactly what Murias meant but hoping if I changed the subject, Hunter would miraculously forget I owed him anything.

"The Otherworld is divided into four cities," Hunter impatiently explained. "We're currently in Murias. You're not squirming your way out of this."

"Where would you even find the ingredients? Or the jersey?" I whined.

My *former* best friend grinned at me and nudged me down a paved path toward a village nestled in a valley. Occasionally, a pretty woman would stop and flirt with Hunter and my initial curiosity soon transformed into wounded pride. "Hey," I snapped as soon as the latest young goddess sauntered away, "what the hell? Am I invisible? No way you're better looking than me."

"I could be," he argued. "Besides, I probably have a natural Celtic musk."

"Dude," I warned. "Don't ever talk about your *musk* again."

He laughed and told me to relax. Nobody was slighting me. "They know you're already spoken for. That's all."

I stopped in the middle of the path, and Hunter kept walking for a few steps before realizing I was no longer with him. "What do you mean I'm spoken for?" I demanded.

He shrugged as if this were no big deal. "Well, you aren't *technically* together now, but everyone knows there's something going on between you and the Valkyrie. That's all."

But this was a *really* big deal, partly because we *didn't* have a relationship and Keira kept stubbornly insisting we couldn't, and partly because *how the bloody hell did everyone know so much of my business?*

Now that I was with Hunter again, I felt like I could throw a few "bloodies" into my vocabulary.

Hunter waved me on, anxious for me to accept my defeat, but I honestly would've taken my chances with the flaming zombie monkey again. I was obligated to remind Hunter he was a tremendous asshole before entering the pub that resembled a movie prop from some film set in the Middle Ages. At least, I *thought* it appeared quaint and old-fashioned, and in a lot of ways, it did, but the big screen TV mounted on the wall at the end of the bar kinda gave them away. And they had a football game on of all things. Not soccer but *football*.

As a linebacker tackled the wide receiver, I recognized their uniforms, and my mouth fell open. "No. Way."

Hunter laughed and held out his hand. "Goibniu, hand me the bag behind the counter, please."

"You have *got* to be kidding me," I muttered.

Hunter ignored me and shoved the bag toward my chest then turned back to the bartender. "An O'Hara's with tomato juice for my friend and a plain O'Hara's for me."

"I hate you," I hissed at Hunter.

"No, you don't," he said.

"At this exact moment? Yeah, I kinda do."

Cheering on the screen made me cringe. I'd already seen this game and knew the outcome.

"Put it on," Hunter ordered.

I groaned but dug the Alabama jersey out of the bag. I groaned again as I slipped it over my head, not because it hurt the knife wound in my back but because Hunter was forcing me to wear a Bama jersey while watching LSU lose to them *and* drinking his disgusting concoction, which together formed what he'd long ago dubbed a "Crimson Horton." Of course, he didn't always know the outcome of the Bama-LSU game, but a few years ago, we'd put a moratorium on either of us issuing this challenge when Hunter and I got into a fight at Walk On's because I'd forced him to wear this very jersey.

I tugged at the hemline and thought about ripping it but remembered this might be my last chance to hang out with Hunter, so instead, I plopped grumpily onto a bar stool and pulled the gross drink toward me. It could be worse. Back home, he'd just serve me a spiked Clamato, which was the most vile drink ever created, no matter how much vodka I put in it.

"How did you even get this jersey here?" I asked.

Hunter kept grinning at me. "I have powerful connections."

"You know, I *am* supposed to save the world and all. Bursting into flames right about now isn't going to help us rid the world of Ninurta and the Forty Thieves."

"Pretty sure you won't burst into flames. We haven't yet, anyway."

I looked around the pub, which had been mostly empty when we'd arrived, but now, it had filled with men and women wearing purple and gold and shooting irate, disgusted scowls in my direction. "How long have you been planning this?" I asked.

Hunter's grin morphed into a self-satisfied smirk. "From the moment Agnes told me she'd brought you here."

"Holy crap, how long have I been here?"

"A couple days. Really, it didn't take that long to get this many people on board. Not much ever changes here, so it gave us all something to do."

I leaned a little closer and whispered, "Why are people talking about Keira and me? What are they saying?"

I felt like a lovesick teenager again, but I didn't care, and Hunter, who knew me better than anyone in any world, already understood this wasn't just a crush or desire to get this perfect woman into bed with me.

"Nobody seems to know the whole story," he whispered back. "Just that you and Keira are as close to soul mates as it gets since soul mates don't technically exist."

I was so startled, I spilled a little tomato-juice-beer on the detestable jersey, which kinda looked blood-stained now, and I thought that definitely improved its appearance. "What are almost soul-mates then? What does that even mean?" I wasn't bothering to whisper anymore. So what if the bartender whose name I couldn't pronounce—or remember, for that matter—overheard my mini-panic attack that Keira and I might have some cosmic connection? Who *wouldn't* freak out after hearing something like that?

"I'm not entirely sure," Hunter admitted. A few of the goddesses I've been hanging out with have told me stories, like Dierdre and Noísiu, and Tristan and Isolde, and let me tell you... those stories *all* have tragic endings. I mean, whatever happened to happily ever after?"

"Why would you think I know anything at all about *any* of these stories?"

"They're these love at first sight kind of myths. So I'd tell the goddess who was sharing this story with me that it doesn't apply to you and Keira, because you two didn't even *like* each other at first. Right?"

"Right," I said, but it was half-hearted and quiet, like I was really trying to convince myself, not him.

Hunter shrugged and continued as if he hadn't even noticed my non-committal response. "At any rate, it's apparently not so much about falling madly in love with someone from the moment you lay eyes on them but about being *fated* lovers."

"Her prophecy," I breathed.

Hunter flashed me a curious look, but Keira's stubborn refusal to allow herself to love me almost made sense now. She'd known from the beginning she'd fall in love with me, but she'd also always known I'd die in battle. And she'd be the one having to escort my spirit home.

It seemed like an unbelievably cruel fate, the kind a person might be condemned to if they'd spent a past life drowning kittens or something. But Keira had always been brave and selfless and kind. She didn't deserve this merciless punishment.

And there was only one thing I could do to protect her from it.

I'd have to pretend like my own feelings had vanished. I'd free her from my constant reminders that I loved her and wanted her love in return.

Because ultimately, I loved her so much I was willing to lose her forever if it meant protecting her heart, even at the expense of my own.

CHAPTER SIXTEEN

By the time we met up with our Norse allies who'd returned from Tyr's funeral, several more days had passed, and I was admittedly reluctant to leave the Otherworld. I thought I'd never see Hunter again, and having the chance to hang out with him and joke around like nothing had changed and the world wasn't really descending into deadly chaos had been nothing short of a small miracle.

But I supposed all miracles had a price, and mine was having to confront more gods and monsters that wanted me dead.

Frey basically abducted me as soon as I stepped into the office building where he'd holed up with the CIA again. Not the *entire* CIA, of course, but a handful of suspicious looking men and women in various death metal or Captain America t-shirts. And I couldn't *not* say something, so what I chose to say was, "Where's Thor?"

"I don't know," Frey answered. "He'll be—"

"No," I interrupted, pointing to the various t-shirts. "I mean, where's Thor? Nobody's wearing a Thor shirt, and his feelings are going to get hurt."

"Gavyn," Frey sighed.

"Hey, it's not my fault he's such a sensitive giant."

The guy in the Captain America shirt glanced between Frey and me and sighed. "Did you have to bring him?"

"Yes," Frey answered. "And Gavyn, stop annoying everyone."

"That's like telling me to stop breathing."

"I'm okay with that," Captain America said.

"Medeina!" Frey exclaimed.

I blinked at him then shouted back, "Marsala!"

Not surprisingly, he blinked back at me and said, "Gavyn... *what*?"

I shrugged and lied. "Thought we were naming Italian cooking wines."

"Like I said," Captain America butted in, "feel free to stop breathing."

Frey rubbed his temples and muttered, "For five days, I didn't have a headache. I'm thinking there's a significant causative factor here."

"Besides," Captain America added, "it's *madeira* wine, and it's Portuguese, not Italian."

I jerked a thumb toward him and told Frey, "I really don't like this guy."

"Medeina," Frey tried again, "the Russian goddess who took over the government has been... neutralized."

"I am *not* adopting CIA slang for assassinations," I argued. "Just tell me y'all killed her."

Frey shook his head though, cutting off my pouty insistence not to be anything like this Captain America wannabe who hadn't stopped scowling at me and was probably wishing he could *neutralize* me. "We didn't do anything, Gavyn," Frey clarified. "A group of Slavic gods and a handful of heroes we trained back in Reykjavik abducted her and handed the government back to mortals then took off. I think a lot of gods were waiting to see how this would play out, and now that one hero has single-handedly defeated—"

"Whoa," I interjected and even held up a hand as if I were about to physically stop him. "I didn't single-handedly do anything. Every battle I've been in, I've had a *lot* of help."

"But you're the one killing these gods. Wepwawet, Menhit, Supay, Berstuk, Asalluhi—"

"Speaking of Asalluhi," Cap interrupted, "the Sumerians are, not surprisingly, pissed off their god of magic is dead. You've got a bounty hunter on your tail."

"And how is this different than any other day?" I retorted.

He shrugged and yawned like this conversation was boring him.

Frey stepped in and explained, "Baton Rouge is empty and will be for a while. All of Louisiana is on edge at the moment, expecting the next city to be theirs. Wherever we go, we're going to bring the Sumerians and disaster. I honestly don't know what to do here."

"I do," I said, and Cap immediately shot me a "Like hell" look, so I flipped him off and very politely suggested he go find a glacier to hang out in for seventy-five years. "We can't go to a populated city without risking countless lives, so we go to an empty one. Let them go to Baton Rouge. What can they do at this point?"

"Even emergency and medical personnel have left," Frey countered. "We'd be cut off from all kinds of help we may end up desperately needing."

"There was *always* a chance any one of us could die, right?" I pointed out. I didn't bring up Tyr and how none of us had thought he'd be the first god among our group to fall.

Frey nodded and went back to rubbing his temples. "Yeah, but if we all die, who's left to protect the world from Ninurta's domination?"

I held up a hand and began ticking off names on my

fingers. "Cadros stayed behind in the Otherworld. Agnes's two sisters are in South America with the Irish heroes helping Mama Pacha and Inti. Freyja and Ull can wait in Asgard, and we'll hole up in Baton Rouge with only two heroes, while Ra and Anubis go after Anhur."

Frey eyed me carefully then sighed again. "Okay, Gavyn. Who do you want with you in a completely abandoned city?"

"You."

"Naturally."

"Joachim."

He nodded as if he'd expected this answer as well.

"Thor, Yngvarr, and Agnes."

"All excellent choices," he agreed. "Plus Keira, of course, but I assumed she was a given anyway."

"No," I said firmly. "Keira's not coming with us."

Frey's eyebrows pulled together in that confused expression of his, and he stammered, "But Gavyn... she *has* to stay with you. Odin's orders—"

"I don't give a shit about Odin's orders. If we need a Valkyrie in our group in case Joachim or I die, send Heidi."

"Who?"

"For God's sake," I mumbled, rubbing my own temples. This whole conversation was giving me a migraine, too. "Just pick another Valkyrie, Frey."

I stormed out of the conference room, believing I'd made the right decision but surprised by how much it hurt. When it hit me that I might never see Keira again, not while I was alive anyway and maybe only in passing in Valhalla, I actually had to stop and rest my hands on my knees like I had to catch my breath. But she would never forgive me for this, even if I were only protecting her.

Because I'd figured it out, what she'd been planning all along with her admissions of taking any chance she could find to save my life.

I'd been assuming she didn't want to get hurt, that by refusing me she was protecting herself. It wasn't her heart she was protecting though. It was *mine*. From the beginning, from before I'd even opened my apartment door, she'd intended to take my place.

She'd always planned to trade her life for mine.

DESPITE SURVIVING ALL the plagues and fights in Baton Rouge, its absolute abandonment still shocked me to the point that I became monosyllabic as we carefully drove toward my dad's house. I mean, where else would we sit around waiting for yet another epic supernatural battle of the ages? Of course, our progress was even slower than the traffic jam incident since the streets were still littered with animal bodies and stalled vehicles.

And just like last time, Agnes complained and insisted we could walk there faster, which was probably true, but why exert all that energy if I didn't have to?

Honestly, I'd perfected laziness and elevated it to a true art form. I was even considering charging admission, like a living sculpture kind of thing, but that would have required planning and effort, and we've already established how I felt about *that*.

My phone rang, disrupting Agnes's five hundredth complaint about our slow progress, and I glanced at the number on the screen then declined the call. Agnes looked between the phone and me and asked, "Are you ever going to talk to her?"

"Go back to your tirade," I replied.

"Answer my question," she said.

"It's none of your business," I snapped.

Agnes grunted at me and folded her arms over her chest

in a, "So this means war" way I'd seen quite a few times. "What the hell happened between you?" she asked.

"Nothing." And why couldn't I think of anything else to talk about so we could change the subject?

"Then why is Róta here instead of Keira? And why aren't you taking Keira's calls?"

"It's safer not to be around me. That's not a secret."

"Odin doesn't know about this, you know. When he finds out, he'll send Keira back. He was adamant she stay with you."

Only Yngvarr and Joachim were in this car with us, so it wasn't like I was worried about the wrong ears overhearing our conversation, but I instinctively lowered my voice and whispered, "Why was Odin adamant Keira stay with me?"

"Don't know," Agnes answered with a shrug.

Joachim, who was driving, hit the brakes as the car in front of us came to a sudden stop, and Agnes hit her head on the seat in front of her, causing her to curse the seat *and* the driver of the other car, who just happened to be her king. Apparently, my short list of allies hadn't quite passed muster, at least with Agnes. She'd insisted we needed another god from the Tuatha Dé, like a showdown without at least two gods from her family was a recipe for failure. So Nuada had joined our crew, although he *still* didn't have a silver arm, which I found terribly disappointing.

"What's up with Bucky?" I asked.

"Lay off the Marvel references. You're going to get us sued," Agnes warned.

"Gotcha," I agreed. "What's up with Rick Allen?"

Yngvarr turned around to scowl at me, but apparently, he was the only 80's rock fan in the group because the reference eluded Joachim and Agnes.

"His name is Nuada," Agnes said as if I'd actually forgotten. "And he doesn't have a fake arm. That's just a story made up thousands of years ago to have an excuse for maimed mortal men not to be kings."

"Maimed Mortal Men would make an awesome name for an 80's rock band," I said.

My phone rang again and Yngvarr helpfully pointed out, "Your phone is ringing," but Agnes snatched it out of my hand before I could decline Keira's call for the tenth time. I tried to steal it back, but the old witch—who was pretending to be a super hot redhead—was ridiculously strong and fast. She not only answered the call, she put Keira on speakerphone *and* told her I was sitting right there.

"Now," Agnes scolded, "tell her why you stuck her with a bunch of second-rate heroes."

"That's harsh," I scolded back.

"Gavyn," Keira sighed, "*what* is going on? Did you have another dream?"

"No," I answered then wished I'd lied about it. A dream involving her and the Sword of Prophecy would have given me a far better excuse for keeping her away from me.

When I offered no other explanation, she added, "Odin is furious. He's sending me to Baton Rouge to replace Róta."

"Why is he being such an asshole about this?" I snapped.

"Because I'm the best warrior among the Valkyries," Keira snapped back. "And if you're the hero who's destined to defeat Ninurta, he wants his best fighters with you."

"But maybe destinies are all bullshit," I yelled. "Tyr had a destiny to die during Ragnarok, but he was brought down by water and bugs!"

Everyone fell silent after my outburst, probably assuming my attempt to force Keira away had something to do with unprocessed grief over Tyr's death. They might have been partly right, but that wouldn't keep Keira away. That explanation wouldn't help her live.

The car behind us honked, and we noticed Nuada had

started driving again. Whatever had blocked his path had been moved, although I wondered why he hadn't just driven over it. We had all-terrain vehicles for just that reason.

It wasn't until we were practically beside them that I saw why Nuada and his passengers had stopped to clear the road. These weren't the bodies of alligators and pumas but humans.

Baton Rouge hadn't become a wasteland.

It had become a cemetery.

CHAPTER SEVENTEEN

I slept in my old bed for the first time in a long while, but the nightmare that woke me had nothing to do with Havard. Instead, I dreamed Keira and I were in a hot air balloon for some insane reason, and flaming arrows were coming at us from every direction. I kept trying to get her to stay down, but she refused and kept standing to shoot back at the invisible archers below.

But her arrows kept bending like they were made of taffy, and by the time she got one nocked, one of those flaming arrows hit her bow, forcing her to drop it. She reached for it, leaning over the basket that had risen so high, I could no longer see the ground. When she fell over the side, I tried to grab her, to save her, but my movements were painfully slow no matter how hard I tried to hurry. And all I could do was watch her fall.

I awoke with a start, my heart racing and sweat beading across my forehead, and my shirt felt soaked even though it was a bit cold in the house. I yanked it off, tossing it on the floor angrily like it had been my shirt's fault I'd had such a horrible nightmare. After pulling on a dry shirt, I didn't feel like going back to sleep so I decided to hit my father's scotch collection. But I hadn't been the only one with that idea.

Agnes sat at the kitchen table with a tumbler and bottle in front of her. She'd been spending a lot more time lately as the young, slightly less scary goddess rather than the cranky and terrifying old witch, and I was pretty sure we *all* suspected it had everything to do with Yngvarr.

"Can't sleep?" I asked her.

"No, Gavyn. I'm actually sound asleep right now but have a disorder that causes me to drink and talk in the middle of the night."

I nodded and said, "I have a cousin with that disorder."

She waited until I sat down to accost me, probably because it made my escape so much more difficult. "Why didn't you send Yngvarr home? You tried to protect Keira, so why not him?"

Oh. Damn it. Of course I loved Yngvarr like my own brother—how could I not? But if I weren't willing to risk everything, or at least almost everything, in order to save mankind from servitude to gods like Ninurta, what kind of hero did that make me?

So I told her, "If I sent everyone I cared about away, I'd be here with just Nuada, and that's only because I don't know him yet."

"Yngvarr's different. Don't pretend like he's just another friend to you."

"Agnes," I sighed, but she cut me off and hissed, "Badb."

"Um..."

"You don't get to call me by your stupid nickname if you won't even do me this *one* favor."

"Okay," I said slowly. "But really, my *staying* here and agreeing to fight for you was kinda my one, *huge* favor. I think you're tapped out on favors from me for the next five thousand years. And besides, Yngvarr wants to stay."

Agnes threw her hands up and exclaimed, "So does Keira!"

"Sh." I glanced over my shoulder into the living room, but Thor, who was really too big to be sleeping on the couch, just snorted then resumed his snoring. "Look, it's different with Keira. It's this prophecy and her stubborn insistence on dying in my place, and how can I possibly fight Ninurta or any of these gods if I'm constantly worrying she's about to sacrifice herself?"

"So instead of talking to her, you decide to banish her? Why do you have to be such a... *man?*"

"Well, I'm pretty sure I was born that way. If not, those doctors did a hell of a job—"

"Gavyn," she groaned.

"What does it matter? Odin's sending her here anyway."

"True, but Yngvarr wasn't part of the original plan."

I poured myself a glass of scotch, which I didn't even like but desperate times and all, and glanced back at Thor's large, sleeping frame. Satisfied he wasn't just faking sleep so he could eavesdrop, I whispered, "So Odin didn't kill Tyr, but I still think he has something to do with Havard and this sword."

"Me, too," Agnes agreed.

"And he'd probably guilt Yngvarr into returning even if we sent him back. He doesn't want us in Asgard."

"He's looking for the sword," Agnes breathed.

I nodded, sipped on my scotch, cringed at the motor oil taste of it, sipped it again, cringed... well, you get the idea. "The real question is what he plans to do with it if he finds it."

Agnes tapped her fingers against the glass tumbler then sipped from it without cringing, which only went a long way in proving she really *was* a witch. "Havard needs to send you more memories," she decided.

"In the history of all things ever spoken, no one has ever said anything so ridiculously obvious."

Agnes lifted a shoulder and said, "At least I've made history."

"Odin's power is precarious," I guessed.

This time, she lifted an eyebrow at me, silently asking if I knew what "precarious" meant.

"It means not secure or firmly in his control, smartass," I snapped. "And maybe Odin doesn't remember everything about Havard and the coup, but he knows he's not as powerful as he once was and *my* sword may help him regain total supremacy over Asgard."

Agnes nodded thoughtfully and looked like she was about to contribute to my rather brilliant theory when her gaze darted above my head and she gasped instead. "Keira."

I spun around in my seat and stared at an angry Valkyrie who stared back at me like she was ready to emasculate me again, only this time, not figuratively.

"How much did you overhear?" Agnes asked.

Keira rolled her eyes and pulled one of the chairs away from the table so she could sit down. "You really think I'm mad about Odin's suspicious behavior?" She reached for the bottle of scotch, and I had a brief vision of her using it to beat the hell out of me. But she only poured herself a glass and, like Agnes, managed to drink it without gagging or wincing.

"I get it," I sighed. "You're pissed off at me for trying to protect you."

"Of course I am," she hissed. "We protect each other, Gavyn. That's what we do, whether we're wanting to strangle the other person or not."

"To be fair, I've never wanted to strangle you. Sleep with you, sure, but—"

"Gavyn," she warned, "don't finish that sentence or I *will* strangle you."

"For future reference," Agnes said, "don't anger a Valkyrie. That whole 'hell hath no fury like a woman scorned' thing is *nothing* compared to a scorned Valkyrie."

"Now you tell me," I mumbled.

Keira finished her glass of scotch and I could see the desire to slam the glass on the table written all over her face, but in a remarkable display of self-restraint, she set it down quietly and just as quietly asked, "Why did you do it, Gavyn? Why did you lose faith in me?"

My voice stuck in my throat. Lose faith? Is that what she thought? How could she *possibly* believe I'd ever lose faith in her?

"Keira," I choked out, but my sappy explanation about how she was one of two people in the entire universe I couldn't possibly stop loving or turn my back on or ever stop believing she could truly save the world was permanently silenced when Thor's large frame suddenly filled the doorway between the kitchen and living room. "I think we have company."

Three chairs scraped against the linoleum floor as we scrambled over each other to figure out who'd joined our slumber party. Thor held a finger to his lips, which were largely obscured by a thick auburn beard, and whispered, "You should know he never comes alone."

"Who?" I whispered back. And, really, when had we fought any of these gods alone? They *all* had their own demigod armies or pride of supernatural lions or—

"Demons," Agnes groaned as she peeked through the window.

I crossed my arms and shook my head. "I told you: I'm not fighting demons anymore."

By now, the others had joined us in the living room, and

Joachim had been attempting to spot either the gods or demons by looking through the same window. But he backed away, telling Agnes, "I don't see any demons, just one guy who seems to be scoping out the place."

"That guy," Agnes explained, "is Nergal, who commands fourteen demons in the western conception of the word."

"Wait," I said. "Does that mean his demons can *possess* people?"

"What about gods?" Yngvarr asked nervously. "Are *we* possession proof?"

"Hey, if I'm going to get possessed, so are you," I insisted, even though I had to work out all the details of dual possession.

"Pretty sure gods and mortals can be possessed by Nergal's demons," Thor said. "And I'm also pretty sure the possession occurs when the host is weakened, so don't get injured. Then again, most of what I've heard about Nergal is just rumor, so maybe it's all wrong."

"And I *always* get injured," I said. "So my chances of getting possessed are extraordinarily high."

"How would we get the demons out of us if we were to get possessed?" Nuada asked.

"Kill Nergal?" Frey guessed.

Thor shrugged. "Never been possessed, so I have no idea."

I looked at Frey and begged, "Can I hit him? Please?"

"Let's not hit the people we're counting on to keep us alive," he responded.

I pretended to think about it then nodded. "Good call."

"So," Keira said. "What do these demons look like?"

"Not sure about that either," Thor answered.

"You're really turning out to be pretty useless," I told him.

"Not the first person to tell me that," he quipped.

"So it's possible these demons look like lions then?" Keira pressed.

We all exchanged a cartoonish moment of staring blankly at one another before pressing our faces against the windowpanes to see the demonic lions. I was actually a little disappointed when it looked like an ordinary lion, although I wasn't really sure how a demonic one would be different. But it would probably involve spinning heads and projectile vomiting and an ability to stalk us while walking upside down on the ceiling.

"I don't think that's a demon," Frey said. "I think it's Zababa."

"Zsa Zsa who?" I asked.

"Zababa," Frey corrected. "He was with the other Sumerian gods during their first televised ultimatum. Haven't heard from him much since then, but I'm pretty sure that's him."

"How can you tell? Do you have some sixth sense that allows you to differentiate between regular lions and gods pretending to be lions?"

"No, I'm just assuming Nergal would be traveling with another Mesopotamian god rather than an Egyptian one, and Zababa is the only one left who can take the form of a lion."

I squinted at him and said, "Damn you and your logic." I wasn't really angry, of course. I'd just been hoping for a better story, like some supernatural magic trick that allowed gods to immediately identify shapeshifting deities. Maybe something in the form of a ring with hidden writing on it that granted its wearer unimaginable power... but at a price.

"So, Zababa, Nergal, and fourteen demons," Nuada sighed. "Remind me again why anyone would think it's a great idea to return to an empty city where our enemies would know we're waiting?"

"It's not a great idea," I argued. "And it's not my fault y'all listened to me."

"From now on," Nuada ordered, "nobody listen to Gavyn."

"Agreed," everybody said, including me.

Nergal and Zababa walked out of our line of sight, so we silently separated, taking different directions of the house to keep an eye on our midnight guests. But once they disappeared around a corner, we *couldn't* find them again, and to make matters worse, some asshole—who may or may not have been me—started taunting us with, "The call is coming from inside the house!"

Of course, that would have just been mildly annoying if I hadn't also been sort of right. As we searched each room and looked through each window, I noticed a few rooms had small areas that seemed colder than the rest of the room. Being the fearless—or idiotic—hero that I was, I decided to check out the strange draft in my old bedroom. As soon as I stepped inside that circle, goose bumps broke out all over my skin, and this time, standing still rather than simply passing through it, I was able to smell the unpleasant odor that had been trapped in this circle along with the frigid air.

But I placed that odor a moment too late.

Sulfur.

I'd walked right into a demon's trap.

And I'd already been possessed.

CHAPTER EIGHTEEN

What can I really say about being possessed? Well, it's me, so quite a lot, but most of it isn't terribly relevant. But since I *did* survive an actual possession—and how many people can honestly say that?—I'm going to share the whole experience anyway.

I didn't even realize I'd been possessed until my body started moving without my permission. One second, I'm standing there thinking, "Oh, shit. Sulfur's a sign of the Devil, right?" and the next, I'm creeping out of my room, my fingers curled tightly around the hilt of my sword like I'm ready to fight someone. But I already knew Zababa and Nergal weren't in the house with us, which meant I was hunting my friends.

My brain screamed at my body to knock it off and drop the sword, but my hands refused to cooperate and my feet kept silently marching me toward my dad's bedroom where I'd last seen Agnes and Frey. If I couldn't control my body, maybe I could at least control my voice. I wanted to scream at them, tell them to restrain me, or hell, even kill me, but I remained uncharacteristically quiet.

That should have been their first clue something was terribly wrong.

As I entered the bedroom, Agnes and Frey hardly glanced at me, and Agnes turned her attention back to the window far too soon. "Did you find anything?" she asked me.

"*Yes!*" my mind screamed. "*A demon, but don't worry, I seem to have him contained at the moment.*"

Instead, my mouth answered, "No."

I felt my muscles tensing against my will, preparing to strike Agnes first, but after all the time we'd spent together and all the battles in which we'd fought side by side, she realized something was wrong before Frey, simply because the demon made the easy mistake of answering her question with a single word.

Who knew my loquaciousness would one day be a lifesaver?

Agnes drew her sword and pivoted with dizzying speed, forcing me to retreat into the hallway. Her eyes blazed with the intensity of a thousand suns, and in a low, frighteningly chilling voice, she said, "Get out of him."

"Badb?" Frey wasn't just confused; he sounded scared, like he was about to witness two of his friends killing each other and had no idea why.

I advanced on Agnes, and she parried then pushed me back into the hallway just as Joachim emerged from the guest bedroom, his bow raised, an arrow ready to sail into his enemy's heart. But I thought he looked strange, almost like there was an orange glow around him, and while his arrow had been pointed at me, he quickly reassessed and released it past my right shoulder.

The arrow narrowly missed Thor, who'd been checking out the bathroom, and he ducked behind the door in case Joachim's next arrow didn't miss.

But the fact that he'd missed at all was as strange as the weird glow surrounding him. Joachim never missed. He was like a freak of both natures—mortal and godly. So it took me a while to figure out he was possessed, too, and that's why there was that strange aura around him, which I didn't see around Agnes or Frey or Thor. But the *real* giveaway that my friend had a demon hitching a ride in his body was that arrow, and my occasionally sloth-like brain began to wonder if Joachim had somehow made the demon miss on purpose.

And if he could gain enough control over his motor functions to skew the arrow's course, maybe I could get the demon Shanghaiing *my* body to become a terrible swordsman, or at least just a passable one. But the whole situation had this surreal quality to it, like I was only watching all of this transpire on stage and I was just hanging out in the audience, stuffing fistfuls of popcorn in my mouth and secretly hoping the hot chick would take off some clothes. When my legs turned me to face Agnes again, or my arms lifted my sword to advance, I *felt* it but I didn't.

And the longer the demon controlled me, the more complacent I became. I was suddenly overwhelmed with this crushing mental fatigue, and my mind wanted to shut down and stop processing, that whole mentality of putting on a favorite series on Netflix and lying on the couch and not moving or thinking or even having to pay attention to the television for a few hours. That's where my brain had gone, and it probably would have stayed there if Keira hadn't attacked me.

She'd somehow snuck up on me and hit the back of my knee with a club, but that's not what got me to fight for control of my own body. I collapsed onto my hands and knees and stared up at this beautiful woman, this breathtaking vision of perfection, and part of me *hated her*. I mean, wanted her dead hated her. I hadn't dropped my sword, so I gripped it tightly in both hands and swung at her leg, but she must've anticipated my move because her blade swung down and knocked mine away.

"Gavyn," she shouted, "I am *not* letting this asshole kill you!"

I think I growled in response, but honestly, I was having a hard time differentiating my own thoughts from the demon's at this point. I tried to get back on my feet, and she kicked me down then kicked me in the stomach, forcing me to double over because demons couldn't exactly escape pain when in a human's body. She was about to club me over the head, most likely in an attempt to knock me out and buy them a few moments to restrain me, when I saw Joachim at the end of the hallway with his arrow pointed right at her.

And by the look on his face, he wasn't planning on missing this time.

I yelled at him, and Keira faltered for a second, which gave me just enough time to spring from the floor and tackle her. We collided into the wall of the narrow hallway as Joachim's arrow whizzed past the back of my head. Any closer and I would have become the Albrecht Gessler to his William Tell.

Don't get me wrong: I wasn't miraculously exorcising the demon just because the woman I loved was in danger. In fact, the demon was really kinda pissed off at me for interfering in the *other* demon's easy kill, but enough of the unpossessed gods descended on Joachim and me in the confusion that followed my interference in Keira's attempted assassination that they were able to restrain us both. The *real* me wanted to know where the hell they'd gotten the handcuffs, but the demon refused to ask. And then I realized they could have gotten them out of my dad's bedroom and was totally thankful this demon was being a stubborn asshole about allowing me to communicate freely.

Joachim and I were tossed into a corner while our friends tried to figure out what to do with us. Joachim just sat there seething, a corona of bright orange flickering around his head, so I figured I'd gotten the more relaxed of the two demons, but the familiar shifting sensation forced me to reevaluate.

"*Havard*," I thought. "*Okay, you bastard. If you're really hanging out in here, do something, would you?*"

After all, it hadn't been that long since I'd found myself Ninurta's prisoner and *someone* had sent me a message via a computer screen. And the list of entities that were both willing and capable of intervening on my behalf like that was pretty short.

I wanted to close my eyes and concentrate, but the demon wouldn't let me. If anything, it seemed to know I was hoping for some divine intervention and kept kicking at the wall to compel my captors to noisily yell and threaten to tie my legs down, too. And just as the demon had hoped, all that commotion made it exceedingly difficult to concentrate.

But lucky for me, and all of us really, I wasn't the one who needed to concentrate.

Keira unexpectedly shouted at our friends and held up her hands to silence them. Her eyes narrowed at my foot, still kicking away at the wall then she gasped, "It's a code. He's trying to tell us something."

"Gavyn knows Morse Code?" Agnes asked.

Keira shook her head as I internally, and metaphorically, shook mine.

"No," Keira answered. "It's not Morse Code. I can't remember *where* I learned it."

"Havard," Yngvarr breathed. "I recognize it, too. It must be from Havard's memories."

Agnes threw her hands up impatiently and demanded, "What does this message say?"

"It's letters," Keira explained. "Old Norse. Not the ancient runes, far younger than that..." Her voice trailed off as she listened to my incessant kicking then she and Yngvarr seemed to decode the message at the same time.

"Kill Nergal," they exclaimed.

My leg stilled as a completely different entity fought for control of my body. Seriously: there were far too many people hanging out in me, which would probably make a good title for a porno but not an autobiography.

Anyway, the demon screamed and cursed and fought against the handcuffs, but Nuada had rounded up some rope, and Joachim and I soon found ourselves hog-tied at the end of the hallway with Yngvarr and Nuada guarding us while the others went on a search and destroy mission. And since I was just lying there, helpless and in a slightly awkward position with a German demigod, I figured I'd try my séance skills one last time.

"Okay, Havard, maybe you're not allowed to directly interfere or something, but come on... at least send me the dream where I find out how to find the sword."

Nothing. Not even a *"Stop talking to yourself, you crazy ass."*

"You're not fooling me," I continued as if the dead god were really just stuck in my brain or something, which actually made me feel sorry for him. Of all the brains to be stuck in, mine was obviously some sort of punishment. Not quite Hell-level but more like purgatory or something. *"I know you're somehow around. Sure, I get that all your knowledge is in my DNA, but that stunt with Sharur and Ninurta and now this? You're doing something to bring up specific memories at just the right time. You know I want to avenge your murder, but you have to help me find—"*

And that's when three simple words formed perfectly in

my mind, in block letters like a warning that could be fatal if ignored.

YOU'RE NOT READY

It might have been my imagination that even the demon froze, surprised and quite possibly a little freaked out, just like me. Why wasn't I ready? And ready for *what*? I already had people trying to kill me and everyone I knew every single day, so sure, Havard, prolong our struggle and let us all get killed like Tyr. A lot of good his stupid sword would do me once *I* was dead and taking up residence in Valhalla.

The longer I thought about it, the more pissed off I got. Havard had already demonstrated he could be a total dick at times, even though that seemed to be symptomatic of all the gods. Even Yngvarr hadn't really cared about Áki's fate until Keira had stepped in and insisted they leave him alone. Asgard clearly had some messed up rules of justice, but our battle now had nothing to do with Asgard... did it?

A door slammed at the front of the house, and Agnes and Frey dragged a battered Nergal into the hallway. "Get your demons out of them," Agnes ordered.

Nergal snorted and pretended he didn't speak English. At least, that's what I assumed he was doing because his response was in some language I was pretty sure nobody spoke anymore. I was also pretty sure whatever he said contained a lot of ancient profanity, which I kinda wanted to learn, but I doubted he was up for a linguistics lesson.

Thor wrapped his massive hands around Nergal's shoulders and shoved him into the wall, growling, "Demons. *Now*."

Apparently, my giant friend had lost the ability to speak in full sentences.

Nergal winced but *still* wouldn't call off his demons, so Agnes just stabbed the bastard with the tip of her sword.

"Havard seemed to think just killing him would do the trick. I vote for giving it a shot."

"And if he's wrong?" Yngvarr asked. "We can't undo death."

Agnes hesitated for a second then shrugged. "If he's wrong, we'll figure out something else. But Anhur and Zababa are still out there somewhere, and Ninurta and Inanna could be in the city, too. Besides, Havard needs Gavyn to get revenge on whomever killed him and his wife, right? If he weren't fairly certain this would work, he wouldn't have suggested it."

It was pretty much at this point that I realized the gods I considered my friends had always known more about Havard's mysterious resurrection in my mind and dreams than they'd let on. Sure, they were initially surprised and they really didn't remember him because of this curse, but they knew *something* about how these dreams and all this knowledge kept surfacing, and for some reason, they weren't telling me everything. I thought back to my original fears that I'd lose myself to Havard's personality and I'd eventually become him if this continued, and I'd largely abandoned those fears after these gods I now considered friends repeatedly assured me that couldn't possibly happen.

But whatever they were hiding from me must be bad, at least for *me*. And I began to suspect I'd made a terrible mistake in trusting them.

Yngvarr took a deep breath and relented. "Yeah. Kill him."

Thor let go of him, and Agnes took a step back then swung her sword at Nergal, decapitating the war god with one smooth motion. The demon inside me squirmed and shouted and cursed, and given the profanity streaming from Joachim, his demon was obviously equally pissed about their boss being headless now. But I quickly lost any interest in what the demons were saying. My entire body burned like I'd actually been set on fire but from the inside out. The pain was so intense, I must've blacked out, because the last thing I remember thinking was, "*I want to die as myself, not Havard. I have to die before I lose myself forever.*"

And then my world, which had become nothing but fire and pain and darkness, burst into a million shards of oblivion.

SOMETHING IS ROTTEN IN THE STATE OF ASGARD

(Shakespeare reference. Nailed it.)

I'd once vowed never to leave Asgard once Arnbjorg and I were married, and yet, only a year since our wedding, I found myself in Midgard again. But it was far too dangerous to meet Tyr at home, so we'd agreed to meet in the realm of the mortals. Yngvarr and Gunnr traveled with me, and by the time we reached the inn where we'd find Tyr and Ull, we were exhausted and filthy from the journey.

Even in Midgard, we had to be careful. Word that we'd all convened in this inn could reach Odin, so we'd rented every room then told the innkeeper that speaking of our presence here would be disastrous for him and his entire village. The inn was warm and smelled of stew, and Tyr and Ull sat by the fire, sipping on tall steins and speaking in hushed voices. Ull's potential involvement in any plot against Odin wasn't terribly surprising since he'd been pushed out of Asgard's court, presumably to make room for younger, more talented gods of war. But I still couldn't imagine why Tyr would turn on the All-Father. This *had* to be a trap, but Yngvarr and Gunnr had insisted on this meeting anyway.

We sat across from them and the innkeeper's wife

brought us our own steins of ale before we sent her away so we could speak privately. "Long journey," Tyr said as if we were simply meeting here for some hunting or other frivolous pastime.

"Yes," I agreed, but I didn't know what else to say. I admired Tyr immensely—he was one of the most honorable gods among the Aesir, and his reputation had cemented my decision to accept his invitation here. Trickery was beneath him.

Tyr took a long sip from his stein then set it on the table so he could wipe his mouth with his good hand. He didn't appear nervous, but this conversation would be difficult for a god whose existence had always been rooted in loyalty and integrity. "A number of gods who have sided with you have asked me to become the new leader of Asgard," he said.

"So I've heard."

"What I want, what I've *always* wanted, is Asgard's safety and prosperity. My utmost allegiance is given to Asgard."

"Everyone knows you serve Asgard above all others," I agreed. "So this meeting... you only want to ensure you'll have my support as the next ruler of Asgard?"

"Me?" Tyr asked, genuinely confused.

"Of course," I said. "Isn't that why we're here?"

"Havard, you've misunderstood. I have no intention of ever ruling Asgard. I've been asked, but it's not mine to rule."

I shifted nervously on the bench and glanced at my brother, who appeared just as nervous as me. But Gunnr recovered her ability to speak first and asked Tyr to explain himself.

"I don't yet believe a conflict is inevitable," Tyr said. "And if it *is* inevitable, if civil war engulfs us, it may be hundreds of years from now or tomorrow. In the event it's the latter, there's something you need to know. *That's* why we're here."

"All right," I said carefully. "What do I need to know?"

"It's about your sword. What did your father tell you about it?"

"Only that it's the most powerful weapon among gods, which makes it the most powerful weapon in any realm."

Tyr nodded as if agreeing with my deceased father but added, "It's older than any of us. No one knows who made it or how long ago, only that it's always been a part of our history. There are secrets only it remembers. There are tremendous power in its light. It whispers prophecies in its bearers' dreams. But its greatest gift to Asgard is that it senses a rightful heir to the throne and grants him the strength to claim it."

I must have stared stupidly back at him for quite some time, but I couldn't have been more dumbstruck if he'd told me this trip had been a ruse to slaughter us after all. Yngvarr cleared his throat and said, "Rightful heir. Then why doesn't Odin possess it?"

"For a long time, he did, but the more he abused his position as ruler of Asgard, the less magic he could wield with the sword until it no longer held any magic at all. His name disappeared from the hilt and was replaced by another, but it wasn't the name of any god he knew. Odin kept the Sword of Asgard locked away so no one could see that he'd lost its favor, but it was stolen—we never learned by whom. No one saw it again until it was given to you as a gift by the goddess, Inanna."

"Inanna?" I breathed. "How did a Sumerian goddess come to possess the sword?"

Tyr shrugged and finished his ale then wiped the foam from his beard. "Odin was furious, but he'd long since made us swear we wouldn't speak of the Sword of Asgard or its purpose. Of course, we didn't know yet he'd lost Fate's favor. We assumed he'd locked the sword away because it was too valuable to risk in mortal skirmishes on Midgard."

"I don't understand," Gunnr interjected. "How did you learn all this then?"

For the first time since our arrival at the inn, Ull spoke. "From Thor. Apparently, in one of his many drinking matches with his father, Odin revealed the stolen sword no longer favored him."

"And Thor told you?" I asked incredulously. He would betray his own father? Sure, I'd grown up hating mine, but Thor and Odin's relationship had mostly been a congenial one.

"Thor told us *after* you were given the Sword of Asgard," Ull continued. "Perhaps your father knew what name had been inscribed on its hilt so he named you accordingly, but it wasn't until we saw the sword's magic return in your presence that we understood the significance of you now openly possessing this sword."

"Odin," Yngvarr growled. "*This* is why he's always harbored a resentment toward our family? If he's planning to hurt my little brother, I'll—"

Tyr held up his prosthetic hand and stopped my brother's tirade before it could properly begin. To be honest, I was a little disappointed. Yngvarr could unleash some epically memorable tirades. "We have no reason to think that. What good would it do Odin to get rid of Havard? That will only anger Fate even more, and he still won't be able to possess the magic of the sword."

"But he *does* know what the sword means, what Havard's *possession* of the sword means," Gunnr argued. "It would eliminate a potential rival for the throne."

Ull shook his head though. "He has no idea we're telling you this now, and he has no reason to suspect you'll ever learn the truth about the Sword of Asgard. After all, there's quite a bit we don't know either, like how Inanna got the sword in the first place and why she gave it to you."

"Our father," Yngvarr and I hissed at the same time.

While Yngvarr's face darkened, I told them about our suspicion regarding the man we'd despised our entire lives. "Inanna was almost certainly one of his many lovers. Perhaps he stole the sword and gave it to her for safekeeping until he was ready for her to return it to Asgard."

Yngvarr snorted and shook his head. "He *had* to have some sort of angle, some way the sword's return could benefit *him*."

Gunnr suddenly sat up straighter and looked over her shoulder toward the inn's door. "My lords," she whispered. "We're no longer alone here."

We rose from the table and reached for our weapons, but the door opened and we immediately recognized the feathered cloak. "Freyja," I said, cautious and suspicious as always when confronted with this goddess. "What are you doing here?"

She pushed the hood off her head and smoothed her hair with one hand while shooting me a strange look that may have signified her own cautiousness and suspicions. "What is this clandestine meeting, Havard?"

"Who says it's clandestine? We're simply here for some hunting."

Freyja scoffed and rolled her eyes at me. "With a Valkyrie? Are you hunting mortal men to fill my hall?"

"Or Odin's," Yngvarr supplied helpfully.

"We're not hunting humans," Tyr sighed. "Havard and Gunnr are old friends, Freyja. He invited her along and as a god of war, he has the right to do so."

Freyja tossed her long, blond hair over a shoulder and shrugged. "You can stick to your hunting story. Makes no difference to me. But I've come on behalf of my brother who speaks for all the surviving Vanir. While we've accepted Odin's leadership, we're not opposed to change, particularly if a new ruler would make our entire family the equals of the Aesir."

"But aren't you?" Yngvarr asked.

"In principle. In practice, you know we're not."

Gunnr slowly let out her breath and sat down. "I never meant to start a revolution."

"That one has begun is simply a testament to how much of Asgard is desperate for new leadership," Freyja replied.

"Who is faithful to Odin?" I asked.

"The fallen in Valhalla will always fight for him," she answered. "And Thor will remain loyal to his father. But we can hardly go around Asgard polling everyone, and I think most are hoping this tension never erupts into war."

"As are we," I quickly added. "I have no wish to see my home in flames. I have a wife and child and above all, I want to protect them."

Freyja lowered her gaze then focused her attention on my brother. She wouldn't look at me again, not after this reminder that my heart belonged to someone else, that it would *always* belong to Arnbjorg. "We all have people we want to protect… except Odin. He loves no one more than he loves power, and that makes him the most dangerous god in Asgard. I believe he can be pacified for a while, perhaps for a long while, but eventually, he will want to punish you for Áki's survival."

"Then I will take the punishment," Gunnr said. "If it spares Asgard, he can have my life."

"Oh, Gunnr," Freyja sneered. "You're so naïve. What does he care about a Valkyrie's insubordination? What he'll never forgive is the challenge by two war gods who stood by your side rather than his. When war comes to Asgard, it won't be the fault of a Valkyrie but the gods who deigned to make her their equal."

THAT NIGHT, the Sword of Prophecy cursed me. I dreamed of Asgard, its lush fields barren and scarred, salted and ruined for generations to come. Flames leapt into the gray sky and ash rained down from the heavens. Color had vanished from my home. The world around me was as gray as the sky.

Somewhere, a baby cried and a sheep bleated, but I was alone in a wasteland. I trudged into Idun's orchard, but all that was left were black trunks. War had consumed Asgard, and I alone was left standing in a world we'd destroyed. I finally noticed a weight in my hand and glanced down to see I held the Sword of Prophecy, which faintly glowed even though no enemies were around. They'd all been vanquished but so had my friends. The light from its blade dimmed, and as I brought it closer to my face, I discovered the hilt no longer bore my name.

And somehow, I knew I hadn't lost Fate's favor; it hadn't decided I was no longer fit to be a leader. My name disappeared because there was no Asgard left to rule.

CHAPTER TWENTY

Keira hovered over me constantly, refusing to leave my room or get much sleep. I guess she was worried once a person had been possessed, any remaining demons might prefer him over possession virgins. Physically, I was fine and kept asking her to get some rest or do just about anything that didn't involve treating me like an invalid for a little while, but she wouldn't leave my side. Finally, about twelve hours after Agnes killed Nergal and freed Joachim and me, I asked her what would happen to the gods and Valkyries if Asgard were destroyed, mostly to get her to focus on anything other than me.

She tilted her head at me, and her eyebrows pulled toward each other as she tried to make sense of my question. "What do you mean destroyed? A slow destruction like what's happening to Earth?"

"No, a fast one like the aftermath of a nuclear war."

"We don't have nuclear weapons in Asgard."

I sighed and tried to push the image of Havard's dream out of my head, but it was lodged in there just as stubbornly as Havard himself. "Yeah, but you have powerful god weapons, right? You can basically cause the same amount of damage?"

Keira sat back in her chair and absentmindedly ran her fingers through her long, blond hair. I watched her as she attempted to process my insane questions and offer me some kind of answer that would satisfy me. She probably thought it was some residual effect of the possession since I hadn't mentioned the latest dream to her. "Asgard isn't as big as Earth, but yeah, I suppose we could cause considerable damage. And we could make large parts of it uninhabitable."

"Right," I agreed. "Like if some asshole salted the fields so nothing would grow."

"People still do that?"

Actually, I hadn't known people *ever* did that. "Well, you still fight with swords and spears and shit, so sure, why not?"

She smiled at me and let her hand fall into her lap. "Point taken. Gavyn, where is all of this coming from?"

I sighed and told her, "Havard had this prophecy where a vicious civil war destroyed all of Asgard and only he was left alive. Except he's *dead* and Asgard was never destroyed, so what the hell does it mean?"

"A warning maybe?"

"That *would* make sense, but somehow, I don't think it was simply a 'Hey, don't lead your followers into a civil war because you'll all die' kind of thing."

"I only know one person besides my father who's good at interpreting prophetic dreams. And there's no way I'm calling *her*."

Freyja. Of course it would be Freyja.

I waved her off and pretended like Havard's prophecy didn't really bother me. "It wasn't really *my* dream, just knowledge of a god's dream, which doesn't mean it's *my* prophecy."

Keira squinted at me and said, "Sometimes, I feel like you speak an entirely different language."

"He's back!" Frey shouted from the living room. Keira and I glanced at the bedroom door then at each other before grabbing our swords and spilling into the living room. I was pretty sure they weren't talking about Nergal considering his body still lay at the far end of the hallway, which meant there was only one other god who could have returned.

"So where was Zsa Zsa when y'all captured Nergal?" I asked Agnes.

"Zababa," she corrected.

"That's what I said."

Thor used Mjollnir to move aside a curtain and peek outside. "Have no idea why he took off or why he's returned."

"I suspect," Agnes added, "he left to get reinforcements."

I was getting tired of playing guessing games, so I joined Thor by the window and tried to find *anyone* standing around outside the house, but I didn't see a damn thing. "Is there such a thing as an invisibility cloak?" I asked.

"If so, I want one," Joachim said.

I nodded because that was every child's dream to have a magical cloak of invisibility, right? And we all knew I was basically a child in possession of my own magical identification card that allowed me to drink.

"Um," Agnes stammered. "I don't think he or his supernatural army are invisible. Just *really* hard to see given they're basically spirits."

"Spirits," I repeated. "Agnes, I swear to God and I don't even care which one, if you tell me he brought more demons—"

"Spirits," she interrupted. "*Totally* different."

"How?" I exclaimed.

"Well," she said but sounded far too evasive, "they can't possess you, so there's that."

"Are these...?" Yngvarr started, but he stopped himself

and glanced toward me like he was afraid to describe them, too.

This time, Joachim threw his hands up, exasperated and in no hurry to discover what *else* demons could do to us. "What the hell is out there?"

Agnes and Yngvarr shot each other a knowing look and continued to annoy us to the point I was ready to kick *his* ass instead of Zsa Zsa's. Meanwhile, the other gods pretended they didn't even hear this argument going on right beside them, and when I turned on *them* and demanded answers, they were suddenly terribly busy scouting out the perimeter of the house or carefully inspecting stupid hammers for tiny imperfections that must have been invisible to the mortal eye.

But Keira apparently had no idea what we were dealing with either, because she crossed her arms angrily and snapped, "Fine. Gavyn, let's just go after Zsa Zsa ourselves."

"Works for me," I agreed, even though I was only bluffing. I mean, I hadn't lost what little mind I had. I didn't want to go anywhere *near* Zsa Zsa's supernatural band of misfits.

But Joachim was far more fearless and slung his bow over a shoulder and actually began sliding locks out of place, first the admittedly useless chain then the slightly more useful deadbolt.

"Wait," Agnes shouted. "Those creatures Zababa has returned with are rabisu."

"Rabbits?" I said. "And why are we worried about *rabbits*?"

"Gavyn," Frey sighed. "Give us five minutes of not being yourself, okay?"

"I'd settle for three," Agnes mumbled.

"Three," I agreed. I set the timer on my watch and waved her on to explain why we were worried about some war god who commanded a legion of rabbits. Seriously, though. What were they going to do? Procreate us to death?

"I *said* rabisu," Agnes continued. "They're more like... vampiric spirits."

I knew my three minutes weren't up, but when someone says *vampiric spirits*, a reaction is just inevitable. "Vampires. Like blood-sucking, stake-to-the-heart, sparkling in the sun *vampires*."

"Pretty sure the sun is supposed to kill them," Joachim offered.

Thor finally lowered Mjollnir and bobbed his large head enthusiastically. "What purpose would sparkling even serve? Is it to force them to hunt at night?"

"Would it matter?" I shot back. "If vampires are faster and stronger than humans, so what if their location and identity is given away by sparkling? They can easily overtake some dumbass trying to run away from him."

"Please stop talking about sparkling," Yngvarr begged.

"I think you should tell us what rabisu actually are," Keira offered.

But Agnes shrugged, which didn't exactly instill a great deal of confidence in me that she knew what she was talking about. "They're spirits who attack humans and kill them by draining their blood."

"But without the sparkling," I pretended to ask simply because this kind of clarification was desperately important.

"Gavyn, if you say 'sparkling' *one more time*," Agnes warned, "I'll feed you to the rabisu myself."

I kinda actually believed her, so I skulked back to Keira's side, hoping she could help me keep my mouth shut for at least the rest of Agnes's explanation.

"We *can't* go out there," Agnes said. "Unlike Nergal's demons, the rabisu shouldn't be able to get inside, but we can't go out there either. I think Zababa is planning on a war of attrition."

"So there's no way to kill them?" Joachim asked. "Even

Hollywood vampires can be killed... a stake to the heart, decapitation. *Something* has to work."

"How do you kill something that's already dead?" she retorted.

"We have to kill the god who controls them," I said. "Like with Nergal or Supay."

"Yeah," Frey said slowly. "There's a bit of a problem with this."

Joachim and I groaned while Frey cleared his throat and blushed a little before finishing. "Zababa doesn't control the rabisu. Marduk does."

"Marduk," I sighed like I had any idea who that was.

"Marduk is..." Agnes bit her lip and her eyes darted around the room. I realized she was scared. *Agnes*: this badass warrior and supreme intimidator, this cornerstone of the Morrigna. And if she were scared, I should be absolutely, unequivocally terrified. "Marduk is complicated," she said quietly. "He's both gracious and vengeful, good and evil, all and nothing. But he is also Enki's son."

I grunted because what else can a guy do when he finds out *two* of the most powerful gods attempting to kill him were related to the same asshole who was *conveniently* pretending to help us?

Joachim, who was basically a smarter version of me, had already reached the whole "backstabbing bastards" conclusion, too, and I *think* he unleashed an impressive tirade of profanity in German, but since I didn't *speak* any German, I just had to use my imagination.

"I say we get Enki over here and see how his son likes watching his dad get the shit beaten out of him," I suggested.

Frey pretended to go along with my dumb idea then added, "Just two problems though. How do we get Enki over here if we can't even leave the house? And just because the rabisu are outside doesn't mean Marduk is, *or* that he'd care about his father's fate."

"*Man,* that family has serious daddy issues," I said. "Besides, how powerful can Marduk be anyway? I'm betting we can take him."

"Think Godzilla meets King Kong," Agnes answered.

"Okay, so he likes to destroy cities. Good news for us is that Baton Rouge is already destroyed."

Agnes decided to ignore me and grabbed Frey's arm as he passed. "Call your sister. Get her to talk to Enki and see if he's hiding anything about Marduk. If he really doesn't know what's going on here, he might able to help us."

"You got it," Frey agreed, digging through his contacts while the rest of us wondered how to survive long enough for reinforcements to arrive. And since I had nothing to offer, I headed toward the kitchen to see if there was any food left or if my dad's squatters had cleaned him out. As I passed by the window over the table, I spotted one of those vampiric spirits for the first time.

Now, I'm not saying I shrieked like a howler monkey in heat, but I *did* react in a fairly unheroic way that likely made even the vampire demons laugh. But those bastards were ugly as hell. I'd glimpsed a tall, pale, bony figure with curved horns protruding from his fairly humanoid face, solid black eyes, a mouth filled with pointed teeth, and a long tongue that protruded between those rows of shark teeth when he smiled at me. And yeah, he *smiled* at me, which was so much worse than lunging at the window or hissing or screaming or pretty much anything else he could have done.

Of course, the dude didn't seem to be male or female. It was completely naked yet lacked any identifying parts, so as soon as Agnes joined me in the kitchen to find out why I'd made that hair-raising cat being neutered sound, I told her, "Go find out if it's a he so I'll know how to talk about it."

"I'm beginning to think there isn't a village in the world that's large enough to accommodate your idiocy."

And because she was right, I completely misunderstood what she was saying and thought she was actually complimenting me, like I wasn't *that* much of an idiot if no village anywhere could claim me rather than being *so* stupid, I'd need a gigantic village with lots of competition for the title. "Um, thanks."

Keira glanced out the window and flinched but managed to keep any embarrassing animal noises contained. A second vampire—which definitely didn't sparkle, by the way—emerged from the shadows of a large oak tree. The sun had almost set now, and I had a horrible suspicion we were about to be overrun by those Mesopotamian bloodsuckers.

"What's our best bet for at least slowing them down?" I asked. "Because if they get inside—"

"They won't," Frey interrupted, but he sounded as sure as I felt.

"Then just humor me," I sighed.

Agnes shrugged. "Never actually met one, but according to legend, they could be repelled with salt."

"Salt," Joachim and I repeated flatly, and for good measure, I reminded her, "I'm not one of the Winchesters!"

"They use salt against ghosts anyway," Keira said. "Not vampires."

"So we have vampire ghosts?" I asked.

"No," Agnes snapped. "No ghosts, just these vampiric demon things, which are undead or never alive or whatever, and since Mesopotamian creation stories claim life emerged from the salt of the sea, it's the purest thing on Earth and can ward off impure things like vampire demons... or some stupid shit like that."

"Salt," I muttered, but I dug through the pantry anyway until I found a saltshaker and a box of kosher salt, although I couldn't even begin to imagine what Dad had needed kosher salt for. I held them up for Agnes to see and asked, "Now what?"

Keira slapped the counter and I could almost see the light bulb going off above her head. "I've got it! We need glue."

I sighed and put the salt on the counter while I complained once again. "Who do you think I am? MacGyver?"

"Of course not," Agnes answered a little too quickly. "MacGyver was practically a genius."

I flipped her off before rummaging through his junk drawer and digging out a half-full bottle of super glue. Keira asked Joachim for one of his arrows, rubbed the glue on the arrowhead, then sprinkled salt over the glue. I had to admit: it was pretty ingenious.

"We should all have bows and arrows just in case they do get inside," Frey decided. He produced a bow from its magical hiding place and tossed it on the table, but by now, the sun had completely set and Baton Rouge had fallen into the peculiar darkness of abandonment. And just as I'd feared, we were about to be overrun with vampires.

Three of them hurled themselves at the kitchen window, which cracked but didn't break. The dumbasses would've had better luck if they'd removed the screen first. Instead, they backed up to hurl themselves at the window again.

Joachim snatched the salted arrow off the counter and nocked it while we listened to windows all around the house cracking. My skin turned cold and clammy—there were too many of them and not nearly enough salted arrows, and that was assuming salt would even work against them.

The window in the kitchen shattered and three shark-teethed, anteater tongued monsters flew into the kitchen, each landing in a crouched position on the kitchen table. Joachim immediately loosed his arrow at one of them while

Keira handed him a second. But so many things were happening at once, it was impossible to focus on just one.

The vampire that had been shot by Joachim's salted arrow shrieked and used his long, bony fingers to pluck the arrow from his chest. His smooth white skin had turned puckered and blue where the arrow had punctured his chest, but the other demon who'd been shot with one of Frey's unsalted arrows simply pulled it out and tossed it on the kitchen floor. Agnes shot the third demon, but her arrow hadn't been salted either. He sprang from the table, arrow still protruding from his shoulder, and landed on Thor.

My stomach dropped as I watched the vampire sink his saw-like teeth into Thor's neck. Blood immediately soaked his collar, but the monster still had his teeth embedded in my friend's neck. Forcing him off—if I were even able to—would remove half the thunder god's neck.

Windows shattered in the back of the house as more vampires poured in. Soon, we'd *all* be dead anyway.

"*Oh, what the hell*," I thought. I lifted my sword and began hacking away at the vampiric demon beast—I still wasn't clear on what they really were—but as I'd expected, my blade didn't do a damn thing. I mean, it left gashes but they healed almost immediately, which really made the hacking completely pointless. And the whole time, Thor just kept pummeling the vampire with Mjollnir, which was as ineffective as my sword. And then there was the bleeding. So much bleeding.

I felt sharp claws dig into my back along with the weight of a vampire the size of a grown man, albeit an unnaturally thin one. Keira screamed and the vampire screeched in my ear but let go of me before my neck could be torn open. I spun around and saw him writhing on the floor, a large blue wound in his back. Keira had salted the blade of her sword.

In hindsight, we should've returned to Asgard as soon as

we realized we'd been surrounded by *vampires*, but now, if my friends opened the veil, these vampires could cross, too. We were stuck in Baton Rouge, surrounded by immortal monsters, one of which was *still* attached to Thor's neck. Keira stabbed it with her sword, and it finally let go of Thor long enough to shriek at her. Most of the salt had come off on the vampire that had landed on me, but at least the one attacking Thor removed his teeth from the god's neck, which allowed me to grab him and throw him across the room.

He sprang to his feet, completely unfazed by hitting the wall so hard the sheetrock cracked, and Frey helped Thor to the back of the kitchen where they pressed dishtowels against the mangled skin. Honestly, it made me too nauseated to look at his neck, so I kept my attention on the vampires.

I counted fifteen of them as we backed into the far end of the kitchen with Frey and Thor. We were cornered. Outnumbered. Walking meal tickets for a bunch of bloodthirsty monsters. Even the vampires that had been injured with salt had gotten back on their feet. *Maybe* we could destroy one if we all descended on it with salt but given our circumstances, that was impossible.

Several of them got within leaping distance and sprang at us. Swords raised and arrows sailed, but a blinding light disoriented us. I squeezed my eyes closed and hoped I wouldn't be permanently blinded then thought I was such a dumbass... what difference did it make if my retinas were burned? I was about to become a vampire's dinner.

The light, so similar to the light in the mystery room in Sumer II, faded and I opened my eyes, ready to at least go down with a fight. But there *weren't* any vampires to fight. In fact, there was *no one* to fight.

We were no longer in my father's house.

I turned in a slow circle, gaping at the mansions all around us, covered in thick greenery like ferns and ivies and, okay, I didn't know a damn thing about plants but they were *everywhere*. Streams of water so clear I could see the pebbles lining the channels that irrigated every last inch of this place wove along the paths and around all those mansions, which were either white marble or some kind of sandstone painted with blue mosaics.

And it was then I began to suspect we'd been transported to a world that no longer existed.

"Where *are* we?" I asked.

I heard Agnes take a deep breath as she lowered her sword. "It's impossible," she murmured.

"It's been that kind of night," I murmured back.

"But Gavyn... this place doesn't exist anymore. We're in Babylon."

CHAPTER TWENTY-ONE

I'd obviously missed the part of our battle against vampires where we climbed into a Delorean, so I kicked at the ground and cursed it before shouting, "We can time travel now?"

Agnes shook her head. I'd never seen her look so confused and helpless, which brought me a giant step closer to freaking the hell out. "We can't. No one can. But I've *been* here before..."

"It's beautiful," Keira breathed.

And it *was*, but if we'd somehow been transported over two thousand years into the past, I had a lot of ass kicking to do. I mean, sure, it wouldn't be Ninurta's for trying to take over the world and everything, but gods were ancient. Zababa had to be around somewhere, so I could do his ass kicking retroactively. Pre-actively? Whatever the word, the ass kicking would be the same.

But Agnes finally grunted at some building about a quarter of a mile from us and sneered, "Marduk."

"He's here?" I asked. "I'll settle for kicking *his* ass."

Of course, they hadn't heard the silent conversation I'd

had with myself about Zababa and his need for a thorough beating, so I got a few strange looks but mostly, my friends just ignored me, which they were getting extremely good at.

"That's Marduk's temple," Agnes explained. "But have you noticed how empty this Babylon is?"

Well, now that she mentioned it, yeah... we did seem to be completely alone. If there were anyone in the city, it seemed like they would have come out of their homes or businesses or temples to at least gawk at these strangers who'd miraculously shown up inside their walls.

"Like I said," Agnes continued, "time travel is impossible. Like Asalluhi, Marduk can also cast powerful spells. We're probably still in Baton Rouge, but he's making us think we're in Babylon."

"Why?" Joachim asked. "His vampire demons were about to kill us. Why bother with this illusion if he's sided with Ninurta?"

"I don't know," she admitted. "But it's the only explanation that makes sense."

"If we're really in Baton Rouge," Keira said, "are we still being hunted by his vampiric demons?"

"We're not being hunted by anything," Thor mumbled. His face had paled considerably, but somehow, the giant god of thunder remained on his feet.

"And *of course* I can't open the veil," Frey complained. "It's like it doesn't even exist here."

Agnes blinked at him then folded her arms over her chest. "It *has* to exist here. It exists everywhere!"

"Can you find it?" he shot back.

For the first time in a long time, Yngvarr spoke. Maybe he'd just been processing the rapid turn of events or maybe he just *really* hated Babylon, but he seemed as pale as Thor although he hadn't been injured.

"Marduk is replicating the city where he was once

worshipped as the patron god, where he was known as a god of justice and fairness. He's evaluating us, judging us. He's trying to decide whose cause to follow: his stepbrother's or his father's."

"So our fate depends on how we act here?" I asked.

"Partially," Yngvarr answered. "I'm sure part of it is also what Ninurta and Enki are telling him."

"We are so screwed," I muttered.

Agnes snorted and patted my shoulder. "Just don't speak again, and we might get out of this alive."

I blinked at her then repeated, "We are so screwed."

"Let's get out of this sun," Frey suggested. "Find someplace where Thor can lie down."

Already forgetting I was supposed to be on my best behavior, I nodded and asked, "Where do you think the whore is hanging out?"

Frey tripped over his foot and grabbed onto Yngvarr's arm to prevent himself from falling. "The... *what*?"

"You know, the Whore of Babylon. Where do you think she is? I suggest we go there."

"Oh, my God," Keira muttered. She kept walking like she'd somehow gotten trapped in a fake Babylon with some annoying dumbass she didn't even know and really didn't *want* to know. Not that I blamed her or anything.

But Agnes apparently decided trying to educate me at least gave her something to do as we searched for a building we could break into so Thor could rest for a while. "Ever heard of Lilith?"

"Sure," I said. "Frasier's wife on *Cheers*."

"Different Lilith. Adam's first wife, Lilith."

"Adam? Like *the* Adam of Adam and Eve?"

Agnes nodded and tugged on a door then pushed on it, but the door remained stubbornly closed so we moved on. "Yeah, his first wife was Lilith but she was cast out of Eden when she insisted on being his equal. Then there are all these stories of her hooking up with a fallen angel and birthing all the demons of Hell."

"Um..." I mean, really, what else could anyone say to something like that?

"Some scholars think she's the inspiration for the Whore of Babylon myth," Agnes continued. "So before looking for her to shack up with for a while, just remember you could very well be looking for the mom of every single one of Hell's demons."

"Um..." Sure, I'd only been joking before anyway, but I'd just discovered that it was absolutely no fun at all to be a *smart*ass around people way *smarter* than me.

Joachim caught up to me and whispered, "If she's wickedly hot, do you think it would matter?"

I laughed and Keira glanced over her shoulder to scold me but got cut off mid-scold when Yngvarr exclaimed, "It's open!"

The heavy wooden door swung toward us, but after Sumer II and the labyrinthine version of Baton Rouge, we were all suspicious of an unlocked building in Babylon 2.0. Agnes called out a greeting in what I assumed was some language a bunch of dead Babylonians used to speak, but only her echo answered us. A water fountain in the center of the tiled room turned on and I thought about heading back to the exact same spot where we'd first shown up here because at least I knew *that* spot was safe, but Frey girded his loins—okay, I don't actually know what that means, but I was in this biblical city and it sounded biblical and relevant—and entered the cavernous room, helping Thor to the fountain where he sat on the edge and struggled to keep his eyes open.

And once two of our friends were inside, we had to follow. We couldn't risk being separated now. Just as I'd been expecting, the door closed behind us and none of us could get it open again. I gave up even trying and stood in the center of the room to take in our new prison. Admittedly, it was a luxurious jail with tall arched windows and a curved staircase ascending to a second floor whose balcony encircled the first floor. All of the doors that lined the balcony were closed and most likely locked so we couldn't enter.

I gestured to the windows and said, "Isn't there a word for when something is out of place in a work of fiction? Like a contrail in a Revolutionary War movie."

"Anachronism," Agnes answered.

"Pretty sure the Babylonians didn't have glass in their windows."

"Pretty sure you're right. They made glass objects but not windowpanes. That's a fairly modern invention."

"You're like a walking encyclopedia," I pointed out.

She smiled and shrugged. "When you're as old as I am, you pick up a few things."

I sat against a mosaic of what may have been a lion or some hybrid lion-giraffe thing, and Frey sat beside me, watching Thor with so much sadness, so much sense of loss. "Seems like we were just here, doesn't it?"

It took me a second to figure out he didn't mean this place but watching one of our friends die.

"Yeah," I agreed quietly. Here we were again, trapped in a hostile world with a badly injured god and no way to get them the medical help they urgently needed. I mean, we were the good guys. Weren't we supposed to win?

And then he said it, what I'd been fearing he believed all along. "Tyr died because of me. He went to Sumer II to rescue *me*."

"Frey," I sighed. "There's not a doubt in my mind that even if he'd known what would happen, he'd decide differently."

Frey kept his attention on Thor but nodded and murmured, "And that's what makes it so painful."

And what the hell was I supposed to say to that? We sat silently for a while, and as I watched Nuada help Thor into a more comfortable position, I became angrier and angrier at the god responsible for us possibly losing another friend. "If you're right about what Marduk is doing," I told Yngvarr, "then he's just sitting there watching one of us die. If he decides to side with his father, he can't undo death, no matter how powerful he is."

"What else can we do though?" Yngvarr asked. "We're trapped."

Thor opened his eyes long enough to say, "Leave me here and look for a way out of the city and beyond the reach of Marduk's magic."

I immediately shook my head and insisted we couldn't leave him here. Even if it weren't possible to save him, we wouldn't let him die alone.

"I agree," Keira said. She'd sat by the god she'd fought with and known for thousands of years and brushed the hair that had stuck to his damp forehead away with her fingers. Agnes had removed her sweatshirt and was tearing it into strips since the dishtowel was soaked through. The bleeding had slowed considerably, but if it didn't stop...

I tried to put myself in Thor's position and knew I'd say the same thing: leave me behind and find a way to escape. Hell, I *had* been in similar situations and my friends had refused to leave me behind, too. Why would he think we'd leave *him*?

"Gavyn," he tried again. "I need a hospital. If you don't—"

And suddenly, I heard myself agreeing with him, only it couldn't have been *me* at all. *I* still firmly believed we shouldn't split up, and we definitely shouldn't leave Thor here. But I almost felt possessed again, like I'd been shoved into some dusty corner in the back of my mind while someone else controlled my body.

Only this time, I knew exactly who it was.

"All right, Thor. I'll go. I'll find a way out and send help," I said.

"*Havard, you bastard,*" I shouted at him silently. "*I am* not *leaving them.*"

But my legs were already rising and nothing I tried made them stop.

"I'll go with you," Joachim offered.

"As will I," Yngvarr said. "Frey, Agnes, Nuada, and Keira can stay with Thor. We'll come back for you all. I promise."

It was a foolish thing to do, promise something when there was so little chance of being able to fulfill that promise. But Havard refused to relinquish control of my body, and we began to search for a way out of the building. After attacking each door and window and discovering they were protected by some kind of enchantment, we ventured up to the second floor, where we encountered the same problem. Door after door refused to budge no matter how hard we kicked and beat against them.

We'd finished our way around the entire balcony and returned to the staircase when Havard had a bright idea. I tried to tell him he was just going to get me killed, but he'd apparently decided that was an acceptable risk. After all, he was already dead; it's not like he could die again.

"I'm going to jump," I announced.

"Jump where?" Yngvarr asked. He paused at the top of the stairs, but I was having a hard time focusing on him rather than the hard marble floor I'd soon be jumping towards. And the second floor of this building was far higher than normal. *What* was Havard thinking?

"Remember that time we... you and your brother..." I trailed off as Havard realized Yngvarr *couldn't* remember him or any of their adventures together. An image, one of Havard's memories, flashed in my mind and he tried again. "You and Havard once got lost in Midgard when Hecate cast a spell on a forest you knew as well as your own fields in Asgard."

"Hecate?" Yngvarr said. "Why was she in Midgard?"

I shrugged and ventured a guess. "She was pissed off at someone. We just got caught in the crosshairs."

"We..." Yngvarr gave me a strange look, as if it were dawning on him something wasn't quite right with this goofy demigod he'd come to know pretty well.

I waved him off as if I'd just misspoken, like I usually referred to other people using first person pronouns, and tried to distract him with the rest of the story. "Everything was reversed. Left was right, up was down. Even after you and Havard figured out why normal directions were so wrong, you couldn't get out of the forest because you couldn't *not* walk, but that's exactly what you had to do."

"So they had to stand still?" Joachim asked. He didn't seem as bothered by my slip up and most likely just assumed it was all part of the bothersome dreams and reliving someone else's memories.

"No," I answered. "They had to go up, which they could only do by going down."

That earned me two blank stares followed by gems like, "That's the dumbest thing I've ever heard," and "Are you sure Havard and I weren't drunk?"

"There was a cliff at the edge of the forest that overlooked the sea, and Havard thought y'all might be able to escape the enchanted forest by swimming beyond Hecate's spell. You both jumped, but instead of falling into the water, you landed back in a forest, *your* forest. The one you knew so well."

Yngvarr sighed and rubbed a hand over his face. "This is a

completely different scenario and a completely different god. There's no reason to think we can escape his spell by doing the same thing."

"Unless all spells are basically the same," I argued. Actually, *I* completely agreed with Yngvarr and told Havard to shut the hell up, but he stubbornly refused. "And I think they are. These gods of magic have the ability to cast them, but the magic itself is all the same, which means the spells are essentially the same."

"Gavyn, we are *not* jumping—"

But Havard gripped the railing on the balcony, gave the frighteningly hard marble one last glance, and jumped.

CHAPTER TWENTY-TWO

When my feet hit the ground, I expected my femurs to break, my ankles to snap, my head to explode. Okay, I wasn't exactly sure what happened to people who jumped off high objects onto solid ground, but I knew it wasn't pretty. But instead of turning into a human pancake, I landed relatively unscathed on the street outside the building where my friends still sat imprisoned. I mean, my left ankle *did* kinda hurt, but I could walk on it, and honestly, I was just happy to be alive.

Of course, my smartass ancestor *had* to tell me, "Told you."

Joachim suddenly landed beside me and may or may not have scared the shit out of me, causing me to yelp and trip on one of the uneven stones that paved the street. Instead of falling, I bumped into Yngvarr, who'd appeared behind me and steadied me before muttering, "I can't believe this worked."

And then Joachim had to go and get all metaphysical on us by saying, "Maybe it's the power of belief. Gavyn was convinced this would work and that's why it did. Once we saw him vanish, we believed it, too, and followed him."

"Okay, then I believe I *really* want out of Babylon 2.0," I said. And this time, it really was me speaking even though Havard was still hanging around. But go figure: we weren't miraculously transported out of Marduk's fake world.

"Well," Yngvarr whispered, just in case Marduk had Superman hearing, "the wall surrounds the entire city, so I guess any direction we choose should lead us there."

"When are you going to learn not to say stuff like that?" I groaned.

"It's a prison," Joachim exclaimed, which led to both Yngvarr and me shushing him. He lowered his voice and said, "It's a prison. We're in the inner cell blocks right now, but what do *all* prisons have in common?"

"Dude," I said, "I've seen *Oz*, and I don't like where this is going."

"Guards, Gavyn," he sighed. "As soon as we step out of the center of the city, someone or something will attack us. It's like reaching the yard when we don't have permission to be outside."

Yngvarr ran his fingers through his hair then shook his head. "Just one kind of something, actually. It'll most likely be a mušhuššu."

"Gesundheit," Joachim and I both said.

"No, that's what it's called. Nobody has a clue what these animals *are*, but they're among the many monstrosities Marduk commands."

"Nice alliteration," I joked.

"Stop using such big words," Yngvarr ordered. "You know that freaks us out." But for obvious reasons, I didn't tell him that hadn't been my ten dollar word at all. And why Havard knew fairly useless English words remained a mystery, even to me.

"Thor needs us," Joachim interjected. "We'll just have to take our chances with the mush..."

The expression on his face made me a little concerned he was going to give himself an aneurysm, so I bestowed the first nickname I could think of on our mystery monster. "Mushy Shoe."

"Mushy...Shoe..." both Yngvarr and Joachim repeated slowly.

"Just go with it. We're running out of time."

"Okay," Joachim agreed. "We've encountered all sorts of creatures already and survived. We'll just have to fight our way past this one, too."

I nodded as we began our trek eastward, which we'd decided on simply because we'd reached this building by walking from the west and we already knew what lay in that direction. A whole lot of nothing. "Of all the monsters we've fought," I said, "my personal favorite is definitely the flaming zombie monkey."

"That *was* a particularly likable evil little bastard," Yngvarr agreed.

"But I was *not* a fan of the devil dogs," Joachim added.

We all grimaced and voiced our agreement that the devil dogs were the worst kind of mutant monsters. We'd walked quite a distance when Yngvarr glanced toward the sky and suddenly stopped. Joachim and I shot him looks that conveyed both, "What the hell?" and "What now?" but Yngvarr's attention remained fixed on the sky.

"Do you hear that?" he asked.

I was about to tell him I didn't hear a damn thing—we were in a literal ghost town considering Babylon hadn't existed in like a thousand years—but as I concentrated, I *did* actually hear something... and it was a shockingly familiar sound.

"Is that a helicopter?" I whispered. I wasn't really sure

why I whispered other than a louder voice might scare the helicopter away.

Joachim blinked up at the bright sky then at Yngvarr and me. "But..." And that was apparently the extent of his objection that we couldn't *possibly* be hearing a helicopter while trapped within a city that took us back to the B.C. era.

"Remember how we were talking about still being in Baton Rouge only under a kind of spell?" Yngvarr explained. "I think we're in some sort of seam."

"Seam," I repeated as if saying the word aloud would miraculously make its meaning clear. And Havard must not have known what his brother was talking about either, or he'd chosen to become a silent observer all of a sudden, which kinda made me want to kick his ass but that would mean kicking my own ass. And thinking through *that* problem just gave me a headache, so I stopped thinking altogether.

"A seam is a place where the enchantment is thin or 'stitched together.' It's weaker here for some reason, most likely because something in the real world is interfering with the magic."

Joachim snickered and asked, "Like a nuclear power plant?"

"Or nuclear waste," I said. "Hollywood likes to blame nuclear waste, too."

Joachim nodded but, really, either one could disrupt magic for all we knew except Baton Rouge didn't *have* any nuclear power plants. The closest one was in St. Francisville, and there was no way we'd walked *that* far.

"What about high voltage power lines?" Joachim asked.

"How do you even know how to translate stuff like that into English?" I asked.

Joachim shrugged. "I'm an electrical engineer."

"Of course you are," I sighed. I really *was* the dumbest hero on the team. "I don't think Baton Rouge has any high voltage power lines anyway. Outside the city limits maybe, but I don't think we've walked that far, have we?"

"I've got it!" Joachim exclaimed, which led to us shushing him again. He grinned sheepishly at us and whispered, "A church."

"A church," I said, just to make sure he hadn't mistranslated *that* word.

But Joachim smiled like he'd just solved the mystery of dark matter and said, "Sure. God's power interfering with *a* god's power. Capital G versus lower case g. Capital beats lower case, right?"

"That sounds like something I would have said, and that's not a good thing, buddy," I told him.

"Please stop talking now," Yngvarr begged.

"What creates these seams then?" I demanded. "If you know, you really should've told us right away and prevented our admittedly entertaining speculation."

"Certain metals," Yngvarr answered. "And while nuclear power plants and churches *would* make better stories, magic is as old as the universe itself. Often, what can be imbued with magic or what can interfere with it comes down to the elements themselves because they've also been around since the beginning, even before us gods."

"But not God with a capital G," I said, mostly just to be a smartass.

"There are all sorts of powers even we don't understand, Gavyn," Yngvarr replied. "But I'm pretty sure I'm right about what's interfering with Marduk's spell here."

"What kind of metals?" Joachim asked. "Maybe we can at least figure out where we really are if it's something pretty rare."

"I don't think we have any golden calves just standing around in our parks," I told him.

"Probably not," Yngvarr agreed. "But iron will do it,

particularly if there's enough of it. And it would have to be exposed. Steel support beams within buildings wouldn't have the same effect."

"Iron again," I sighed. I tried to think of any construction near my dad's neighborhood or anything else that might be made of exposed steel. A refinery? Most of those were by the river, and we weren't close to the Mississippi. A warehouse? I was pretty sure they were made of cheaper metals like aluminum. A train?

"Train tracks," I breathed. Yngvarr and Joachim both arched eyebrows at me, so I quickly explained my hypothesis. "I'm pretty sure we were still at my dad's house when we found ourselves in Babylon 2.0. Marduk just switched what we think we're seeing, right? So if that's the case, between walking to the building where our friends are trapped and the distance we've walked since leaving their prison, we should be out of his neighborhood. And there are train tracks about three miles outside of that subdivision. And it also means that if I'm right, I know exactly where we are."

Yngvarr hesitated only a moment before extending his arm and telling me to lead the way. I noticed the streets between buildings were no longer straight but curved and would occasionally form unusual patterns, like they were following an unchangeable path rather than the streets accommodating the structures around them.

For the first time since arriving in Babylon 2.0, I was beginning to feel optimistic that we might find a way out. I should have known better than to think something like that, but what can I say? I'm a slow learner. We heard it for the first time shortly after that traitorous thought popped into my head, this cross between a lion and a dragon and maybe even a bit of eagle... just for good measure. "Um," I stammered. "Mushy Shoe?"

"I'm thinking yes," Yngvarr whispered.

"Why are you whispering again?" I whispered back. "They already know where we are."

"Why are *you* whispering then?" he continued to whisper.

"You started it."

Joachim pulled an arrow from his quiver and turned in a slow circle. The beast made that blood-curdling sound again, but either the buildings or the monster itself were playing tricks on our senses. We each thought the sound was coming from a different direction.

A blur of colors—blues and yellows and reds—flashed in front of me and was gone as quickly as it appeared. I held my shield out, just in case it decided to leap at me from its Houdini-level hiding place. But Joachim announced *he'd* seen the monster, too, and considering we were facing opposite directions, there was really only one explanation for why.

"Mushy *Shoes*," I complained. "Of course, there are multiple monsters. Why would we ever catch a break?"

Our Mushy Shoes apparently thought that was an invitation to attack us. From every intersecting path between the buildings where we'd been sandwiched, strange beasts emerged with the bodies of dragons, the hind legs of an eagle's talons, the forelimbs of a lion, and the head and neck of... well, I didn't have a clue *what* their grotesque heads were modeled after.

The bright blue and gold scales that covered their bodies reflected light from the setting sun, and the Mushy Shoe squaring off with me made that screeching, roaring, hyena-laughing sound. And that's when I discovered it also had the tongue of a snake.

"Oh, these bastards *have* to die!" I shouted.

Joachim released the string on his bow and an arrow flew toward the Mushy Shoe facing him, but as I'd feared, the dragon scales covering its body were clearly out of a J.R.R.

Tolkien novel. Mushy Shoe didn't have jewel-encrusted armor or anything—its scales were just that impenetrable.

"We'll have to decapitate them," I said. "Joachim, you *do* have a sword, right?"

Yngvarr handed him a sword, at which Joachim actually wrinkled his nose, and we braced ourselves for the attack of the Mushy Shoes. I decided that would be a great name for a not even B level horror movie, so I told them that and got a couple of "shut ups" with some colorful language thrown in.

The Mushy Shoe in front of me shook itself, kind of like a dog drying off, and wings unfolded from its scaled body. Despite its dragon and eagle hybridization, I hadn't been expecting its ability to *fly* so when it took to the air and screeched toward me, I screeched back and took to the streets. Yngvarr and Joachim followed close behind me as we ducked into a narrow alleyway, hoping we could at least force them back on the ground where we stood a shot of cutting off their grotesque, horned heads.

Instead, they formed a single line and flew into the alleyway.

And, unfortunately, Mushy Shoes weren't stupid. They used their talon-like hind legs to try to decapitate *us*. We slashed at them as they dipped from the air, but aside from a few minor nicks, their legs were unscathed and we were hopelessly stuck.

The Mushy Shoes circled above us then darted back towards the ground. I quickly added decapitation by a flying dragon-lion-eagle-snake monster to my list of unacceptable ways to die and was trying to figure out how to survive the next few seconds when a fire unexpectedly ignited right in front of us, its flames reaching so high, it obscured the tops of the buildings we'd been sandwiched between.

But the Mushy Shoes, those freaks even by mythological standards, obviously weren't flame retardant because they screamed and flew wildly as they temporarily turned into phoenixes. I couldn't see where the monsters landed—or, more accurately, fell—but as soon as their headache inducing screaming stopped, the fire died, and there, at the end of the alleyway, stood a god I'd never again resent for being so damn good looking that Keira might decide she could do way better than me.

"Ra?" Yngvarr said. "What... how the hell did you get here?"

"I've *been* here," he said. "One minute I was in Baton Rouge pursuing Anhur, the next I'm in Babylon. I mean, *Babylon*."

"And Anubis?" Joachim asked.

"Here," he called from the street. We peeked around the corner of the building, and he offered us a small wave like we were just running into each other on our way to the Spanish Town Mardi Gras parade.

"Any chance *you* know the way out of Babylon 2.0?" I asked him.

Anubis lifted a shoulder and hazarded a guess. "Over the wall?"

"Have you reached the wall?"

"Um... no. We keep ending up back here, which is pretty much where we started when we first came here."

"Of course," I sighed.

"Did you hear the helicopter?" Yngvarr asked Ra.

"Yeah, must be a seam," he answered matter-of-factly. I mean, what dumbass *wouldn't* know about seams? But then I remembered I was supposed to like the guy now so kept my mouth shut in case those Mushy Shoes returned. For all I knew, they really *were* part phoenix and could be reborn soon.

But *then* I had a legitimately brilliant thought, and it *was* my thought and not Havard's. "If we can't get through the wall, maybe we can find one of these seams where the magic is so weak, we can break through it."

"I still think the wall is the safer bet," Yngvarr argued. "Thor's running out of time, and we don't even know if a seam like that exists."

"Wait," Ra interjected. "What's wrong with Thor?"

"Uh, we may have been attacked by vampires. Some more so than others."

Ra blinked at me for a few seconds before repeating, "Vampires."

"Yeah, they have some other name, but that's basically what they are."

"Rabisu," Yngvarr supplied helpfully.

"Those," I said. "Ugly bastards, too."

Ra massaged his forehead, and for the first—but certainly not the last—time, I began to wonder if I'd manage to give every single god in the world a splitting migraine. It was a lofty goal, but I was up to the task.

"Assuming we're able to get back to Baton Rouge," he said, "the rabisu are probably waiting for us. And since they're essentially demons, we can't kill them."

"*Man*, I've had enough demons for one day," I complained.

Ra arched an eyebrow at me so Joachim announced, "Oh yeah, we got possessed, too."

The sun god looked from Joachim to me to Yngvarr to Anubis and made his own announcement. "I should've stayed home."

"Rebar," I said, which earned me four strange looks since I'd provided no context whatsoever. "Well, it's made of steel, right?"

"Yeah," Joachim answered. "Do you happen to have a sizeable stash of it somewhere?"

"No, but I *do* know where a company that stores and sells it is, and it *should* be within the confines of Babylon 2.0. The more obvious choices like the new bridge over the river would be beyond the walls. I think Marduk was pretty careful in configuring his prison."

"What did I tell you about using big words?" Yngvarr teased.

We learned something else about Babylon 2.0 then. Apparently, we really *couldn't* kill monsters here. Not permanently, anyway. The screeching of Mushy Shoes returned along with the flapping of wings, and we wisely decided to run. I tried to keep up the mental map of Baton Rouge so I'd know where to turn and when, but it was damn near impossible to travel a city that looked nothing like the actual city. We had to rely on both my instincts and the number of Mushy Shoes that followed us, assuming the closer we got to the weakest link in Marduk's spell, the more monsters he'd use to stop us.

But Ra's ability to draw power from the sun, even if it weren't the *real* sun, came in handy again. Each time a Mushy Shoe got too close to us, he turned it into a steaming pile of fried chicken, and the others would drop back, thinking *they* didn't want to be turned into a steaming pile of fried anything. Their memories, however, must have been fairly short, because ten minutes later, another one would get too close and burst into flames.

By that point, I'd become convinced Thor was already dead. Poor guy had just lost his best friend, and now, we hadn't been able to save him. I was pissed and frustrated and ready to kick *some* god's ass, and I wouldn't have been picky about whose, when I heard the convoy. My allies stopped running, and for good measure, Ra torched the Mushy Shoes that had been pursuing us, just in case they decided to attack us while we followed the sounds from what may have been armored vehicles rolling through the streets of Baton Rouge.

The screaming of the Mushy Shoes temporarily disoriented us, but as they quieted—really, not even mythological monsters can still scream when they've turned into ash—we picked up the murmuring of a slow moving parade of Humvees. "We're still in Babylon 2.0," I complained. "Should we click our heels and insist there's no place like home?"

Joachim pointed to my shoes and said, "They aren't ruby. I doubt it'll work."

"They're supposed to be silver anyway," Yngvarr said.

"You've never seen the movie, have you?" I asked.

"You've never read the book, have you?" he shot back.

"Would you shut up about *The Wizard of Oz*?" Ra snapped.

"The book is called *The* Wonderful *Wizard of Oz*," Yngvarr mumbled, but he promptly acquiesced when Ra shot him an admittedly intimidating scowl.

Anubis, who often wisely abstained from our ridiculous arguments, lifted a hand and pointed to the sky. "What do you think that is?"

I looked up at the still bright, midday sky—because, apparently, time stood still in Babylon 2.0—and noticed the purple, rippling gash in the otherwise cloudless, perfect heavens. "What the hell?" I murmured.

"The Humvees," Joachim breathed. "The more that roll into the city, the weaker Marduk's magic will become."

"We must also be close to this rebar place Gavyn mentioned," Yngvarr said. "Not sure either of those things alone would be enough to cause a rift in the spell, but if we follow the convoy, we might find one."

And really, that was a better idea than standing around arguing about the color of Dorothy's slippers, so we kept pace with the procession, which grew louder and louder the farther we walked. We almost lost them a couple of times as they turned on streets that weren't visible to us, but we finally found what we'd been desperately searching for: a rippling, purple gash low enough for us to enter... not that any of us *wanted* to be the guinea pig who walked through it first, but if someone didn't suck it up and venture into what may have been a doorway back to Baton Rouge or a portal to another galaxy, we'd really just wasted time and let Thor die for no good reason.

So I took a deep breath and offered to go first, which led to Yngvarr trying to stop me and take my place, which led to Ra muttering, "Oh, for God's sake, *I'll* go," and stepping into the purple portal thing before anyone could offer to take *his* place.

"I suppose I shouldn't leave him wherever he is," Anubis said, eyeing the purple gash like it would transport him to some place *truly* horrible... like Tuscaloosa.

"It better not be Oz," Joachim said.

"It better not be Sumer II," I added.

Joachim nodded just as the screeching of the Mushy Shoes resumed. "Our phoenixes are back, and our sun god just stepped through the rift. Pick your poison: monster freaks or potential destruction by a rift in space and time."

Yngvarr and I hesitated only a second before we both answered, "Rift."

And we stepped through the doorway into a Baton Rouge under siege.

CHAPTER TWENTY-THREE

Blackhawks swarmed overhead like hummingbirds on steroids and Humvees and *tanks*, actual *tanks*, lined the streets, stretching so far in every direction, they seemed to have an endless supply of vehicles that could blow us out of Louisiana. Hell, out of the country, for that matter.

Khaki-clad soldiers spotted us right away and raised their rifles at us, shouting at us to get down except with a few inventive obscenities thrown in, just in case we didn't speak G-rated English. The gods looked around, completely unconcerned about the soldiers' threats since bullets couldn't harm them, but Joachim and I immediately complied while our dumbass friends just stood there, taking in the war zone my hometown had become.

"Young man," Ra called out to one of the soldiers pointing a rather deadly looking rifle at us, "what is happening here?"

I really shouldn't repeat what that young man said, but it was along the lines of, "None of your business, good sir. Now, if you'd be so kind as to get on the ground."

But here's the thing: gods, even the good ones, don't like mortals ordering them around, and they especially don't like being ordered around with so much condescending attitude. Irritated, Ra waved a hand toward the Humvee behind the disrespectful little shit... er, I mean, the young soldier just doing his job... and it exploded in a fiery inferno that sent the charred skeleton of the vehicle far into the air.

Miraculously, no one was hurt. Or not so miraculously, really, since Ra had the ability to control fire and could choose if he wanted someone or something to burn, but since I had no idea how any of that worked, I was sticking with miracle. Of course, after blowing up one of their vehicles, the other soldiers who hadn't dived into the asphalt to escape the flying debris opened fire on the gods. Joachim and I tried to press ourselves flatter into the ground, which didn't work, by the way, and the gods just waited for the soldiers to either realize shooting these strange men wasn't working or run out of bullets.

I kinda wanted to see what it looked like to shoot a god, but I also kinda didn't want my head to get blown off, so I waited until it got quiet before turning my head just enough to shout at Yngvarr. "Think you can explain who we are now so Joachim and I can get up and we can get on with finding Marduk so we can get our friends out of Babylon 2.0?"

"Oh," Yngvarr said. "That's probably a good idea."

I sighed, "Dumbass," into the ground, and I had the strong sense that Havard totally agreed with me.

Yngvarr and Anubis took turns explaining we were the good guys, the ones risking our lives to stop Ninurta and the others from executing their supernatural coup. The soldiers finally allowed us to get up after they verified *my* identity. Apparently, I'd become the face of Earth's rebellion, which was just *fantastic* news for anyone who ever knew me... like my ex-girlfriend. How many ex-girlfriends and former roommates and grade school friends were Ninurta and his minions going to dredge up? Having known me had become a curse. You know, even worse than the previous one where having known me just meant you'd once had to associate with me.

One of the officers approached me, looking a bit nervous, but I doubted he was nervous about *me*. I imagined this guy had seen combat in at *least* one foreign country, but nothing could ever really prepare a person for going to war with gods. "We, uh, we've got a few folks on the way that've been looking for you."

Okay, maybe this guy *did* want me dead.

"Who?" Yngvarr asked. The tone of his voice startled me. Sometimes, having Havard's sense of brotherly love and familiarity made it easy for me to forget he was a powerful god of war.

"A handful of gods who're on your side," the officer answered.

Well, that didn't exactly narrow it down. Cadros? Agnes's sisters? Ull?

"They came to town with us," he explained. "They'll be here soon."

As if on cue, a motorcade slowly wove through the crowded street and stopped in front of us. One of the doors opened almost immediately, and a tall man with an olive complexion and neatly trimmed beard stepped out. I'd never seen this guy before in my life, but the gods knew exactly who he was.

"Marduk," Ra growled. He stepped forward, but Anubis grabbed his friend's arm to stop him, while Marduk held up a hand in that universal symbol of, "Dude, peace. I didn't come here to fight."

I wasn't really surprised when Enki and Ninhursag got out of the Humvee next.

"Where are the others?" Ninhursag asked. "And where have you been?"

"Why don't you ask your son?" I snapped.

"Which one?" Enki asked.

I grunted at him and waved a hand toward Marduk.

"Me?" he said. "I'd been *trying* to stay out of this whole mess until someone stole the rabisu. I had to come to Earth to track them down and send them back to their prison, but I haven't seen a man or god here in Baton Rouge since."

"Because you sent us to Babylon 2.0!" I shouted.

"I... don't even know what that means," he claimed.

"Gavyn," Enki said, "where are the rest of your colleagues?"

"Haven't you been listening? They're in Babylon, except not *the* Babylon, of course, but a replica of the city that exists parallel to this one. We crossed back into the real world when all these steel-covered vehicles came into town, allowing the magic to get weaker."

"Your brother," Enki hissed.

"*Step*-brother," Marduk corrected.

Enki flicked his wrist at his son like it was a minor detail.

"But," Yngvarr said, "Ninurta isn't a god of magic. And Asalluhi is dead. Isn't he?"

"Yeah," Enki replied. "Ninurta must've had help. Who's still out there?"

"My son," Ra said. "But he can't perform magic either."

"Zababa," I offered. "We assumed he was the one attacking us with the vampires."

"Quite likely," Marduk agreed.

"That leaves Ninurta and Inanna, right?" Ninhursag asked.

"Both war deities," Yngvarr said. "They clearly have an ally we don't know about."

"Allies," I breathed. "Marduk, you have to figure out how to get our friends out of Babylon 2.0. If Thor isn't dead already, he's got to be on death's doorstep."

"Shit," he sighed, but he also looked like he was concentrating, so I didn't ask him if that meant, "Shit, another dead god on our side," or, "Shit, this is one tricky spell and I probably can't undo it."

But about half a minute later, he nodded and pulled his cellphone from his pocket. "Who's with him?"

"Frey, Keira, Nuada, and Agnes," I said.

"Frey, Nuada, who, and who?"

"Just let me call," Yngvarr said. "It'll save us all valuable time."

Yngvarr dialed Agnes's number, which he'd already memorized and I found *that* kinda telling but decided to rag on him about it later. With the spell broken, Agnes went outside to describe her surroundings so we could get an idea of where to find them then a handful of soldiers loaded us into two separate Humvees and drove us back toward my dad's neighborhood.

Miraculously, Thor was still alive. He was drifting in and out of consciousness but alive, and our new Army or National Guard friends—okay, I wasn't quite sure what branch of the military they were from and I hadn't thought to ask—had already called in a medical transport. I fidgeted with the leather strap on my shield the entire ride, just repeating his name and Tyr's in my mind and remembering how infinitesimal I'd felt when I watched my friend collapse, Agnes administering CPR, *knowing* already I'd never speak to him again but hoping and praying for the impossible anyway.

The impossible hadn't happened for my mother and it didn't happen for Tyr either.

But this wasn't impossible. Thor was alive. Maybe someone could save him.

"There is some good news," Enki offered.

I glanced at him then promptly returned my attention to the leather strap. "Yeah?"

"No new takeovers or long forgotten gods emerging from long forgotten kingdoms to make a bid for power they no longer deserve. Perhaps this tidal wave is slowing down as gods wait to see how it will play out with the Sumerians."

I snorted but it was a snarky snort—a snart? a snorty? "What makes you think any of you *ever* deserved the worship of mortals?"

"I can't blame you for your cynicism, Gavyn," Enki said. "But some of us really tried to help humankind."

Since meeting him, Anubis had struck me as a quiet god, but now, he was not only quiet but kept glancing in my direction then averting his gaze as soon as I noticed. I waited until he was focused on staring at the backs of his hands again before nudging Yngvarr with my elbow and nodding toward the peculiar god.

Once Anubis realized Yngvarr was watching him, too, he stopped trying to steal glances in my direction.

Agnes waited outside the house—the totally normal, two-story, antebellum inspired home—and urged the two medics who'd ridden in the other Humvee to follow her. The helicopter circled above us, looking for a suitable place to land, and I twisted then untwisted that leather strap over and over until my fingers blistered. Finally, the chopper landed and four more medics jumped out, pulling a gurney behind them. I had the crazy thought that there was no way Thor would fit on that stretcher, but I didn't stick around to find out. I *couldn't*.

"Call me when everybody's ready to leave," I mumbled in Yngvarr's direction. He wanted to go with me, but someone stopped him. Even before he caught up with me, I knew who it would be.

"You're acting even stranger than usual," I told Anubis.

"Am I? I wasn't aware I normally acted so strange."

I lifted a shoulder and said, "Probably part of being a god of the dead."

"Probably," he pretended to agree.

"How have you gods done this for thousands of years? Everybody within a pantheon is somehow related, and fathers and sons are just out there okay with killing each other."

Anubis was quiet for almost an entire block as he thought about his response. I guessed my question wasn't exactly an easy one, or all that fair since I shouldn't have expected him to have all the answers about supernatural behavior. "I suppose," he said, "it's not so different than when powerful dynasties ruled over kingdoms on Earth. People intermarried, killed parents or siblings or sons... power is the most dangerous weapon in the world, Gavyn."

"And Ra? When he finds Anhur, what will he do?"

"Try to take him home and deal with him in our world by our laws."

"And if he can't?"

"Then it won't be the first time he's had to deal harshly with a child."

Yngvarr called me to let us know the medics had loaded Thor into the helicopter and were about to take off. The god of thunder had been awake when they brought him out, and he'd smiled at his friends and offered a weak thumbs-up, and I felt incredibly guilty for not being there. But Yngvarr refused to let me whine about it, insisting the trauma we were all experiencing affected us each differently and we shouldn't apologize for dealing with it the only way we could.

I disconnected and suggested we at least power-walk back, but Anubis did the exact opposite: he stopped. "Gavyn, I didn't want to mention this in front of the others because I could certainly be wrong. In fact, I hope I *am*. It's just a spell of this magnitude, to convince a bunch of demigods and gods that they were in Babylon... I doubt even Isis could pull off something like that. Asalluhi could have, but we're *sure* he's dead?"

This had been bugging me as well. If that bastard had somehow survived...

"I guess his death could've just been an illusion," I said slowly. But if Asalluhi *was* alive, then Marduk, Enki, and Ninhursag had been a part of the deception and had done a remarkable job of fooling us all.

"But let's assume Asalluhi is dead. When we were in Babylon, we all thought Marduk had cast the spell," Anubis said. "And it *would* make sense. Babylon was his city. He controls the rabisu that attacked your group in Baton Rouge, and even the Mushy Shoes are associated with him."

"But?"

"But I don't think he was lying. Do you?"

I thought about it, how genuinely puzzled and surprised he'd seemed when we accused him of sending us to Babylon 2.0, and sighed. "No, I don't think he was lying."

Anubis nodded and looked around the empty neighborhood like we were spies about to reveal top-secret information. "There are few gods anywhere in the world that could have accomplished such a monumental deception."

I was beginning to get a headache from all the insinuations and baiting. "Just tell me who you think is behind sending us to Babylon 2.0," I snapped. "My friends are waiting on me."

Anubis took a deep breath and raked a hand through his hair. "It's only a suspicion, Gavyn. Technically, two. There are *two* gods capable of doing something like this. And they're both in your pantheon."

"Mine?" I said, a little too defensively at first considering I'd had my doubts about some Norse gods all along, and Keira and I *knew* there had to be a traitor involved in Havard's death. But for some reason, hearing that same suspicion from an outsider irked me.

But Anubis nodded and surveyed the neighborhood one

last time before whispering, "You already know who they are."

And I did. I already knew *exactly* who they were.

"Freyja," I whispered back.

Anubis nodded.

The next name stuck in my throat, and I had to force it out, erupting like some cross between a croak and a whimper. "And Odin."

"And Odin," he repeated quietly.

So this was it then. Zero hour. One of our own, or maybe both of them, wanted us dead.

Power is the most dangerous weapon in the world.

And I knew, I'd always known, who had betrayed us once and who would do it again, just as I knew why he'd spared my life with the rabisu. He needed me to lead him to the Sword of Asgard. As long as it was in his possession, no one could dethrone him.

And Odin would slaughter anyone who attempted to strip him of his power. In the end, he would murder me.

THE END IS NIGH

(And why doesn't anyone say "nigh" anymore?)

Astrid's first steps took me by surprise. We'd recently celebrated her first birthday, so it wasn't her age but simply my inability to accept how quickly my firstborn child was growing up. Arnbjorg had recently learned she was expecting our second, and we sat in the nursery watching Astrid pile blocks then knock them down, and even though she was knocking them down herself, she'd cry each time before rebuilding.

"Our daughter is rather fickle," I told Arnbjorg.

"She's preparing for her life as a woman," she teased.

I arched an eyebrow at my wife but knew better than to agree. And that's when it happened. One of her blocks had landed next to my foot, but instead of crawling toward me to retrieve it, she pushed herself unsteadily to her feet and took her first shaky steps.

Our celebrating, though, was soon interrupted when Gunnr and Áki appeared in the doorway. "Alert Asgard," I laughed. "Astrid is walking and ready to conquer."

Gunnr laughed, too, but Áki looked confused. "But she's still a baby," he insisted.

The Valkyrie placed a hand on his shoulder and instructed him, "Help her build a castle while I talk to my friends."

Áki had kept his distance from Astrid at first, seemingly afraid of how easily she cried and afraid we'd blame him for mistreating her, but for the past few months, with our daughter growing into toddlerhood, he'd taken more interest in her and proved to be as gentle a playmate as he was skilled on the battlefield.

And on numerous occasions, I'd found myself admitting to Gunnr my deep regret that I'd ever ordered her to kill this child whose heart was both fierce and kind, and whose mind was as sharp as it was spirited.

Gunnr led Arnbjorg and me to the library next to the nursery and her expression immediately shifted from that of the happy, doting mother to that of the terrified, anxious one.

"What is it?" Arnbjorg whispered.

"Odin," Gunnr whispered back. "He's left Asgard."

Arnbjorg and I stared blankly at our friend. *Left?* Wasn't he *always* leaving Asgard to rendezvous with whatever lover he'd taken at the moment?

"Too many gods have allied with you and Tyr," Gunnr continued. "He won't rely solely on the fallen in Valhalla. We think he's recruiting help elsewhere, but what he's promising, who he's conspiring with… we were unable to learn any of the details, my lord. But none of us could find him in Midgard."

"So he plans to return with an army," I sighed.

Arnbjorg glanced over her shoulder at the wall the library shared with the nursery. I knew her fear. I felt it myself. "How long?" she asked.

"It could be quite some time yet," Gunnr answered. "The world of gods moves at a different pace than the world of men. When we're not limited by the passing of time, we have the luxury of waiting as long as we need to. He won't return until he's confident he can win."

"Then we must prepare and become confident of our victory as well," I said.

"He means to kill you, Havard," Gunnr whispered. "We will *all* pay for our rebellion with our lives."

"Only if he wins," I argued.

She nodded slowly as a delighted squeal from the nursery returned smiles to our faces for the first time since Gunnr brought us into the library to deliver the news we'd been expecting. I wrapped my arms around my wife and kissed her forehead, thinking a hundred years could pass, five hundred, a thousand, and it still wouldn't be enough.

"We'll lose," she mumbled into my shoulder.

"Yes," I told her, stroking her golden hair.

"He'll kill everyone, Havard. Our children, the Valkyries, your brother and mine, your sisters, our friends... everyone we love."

I continued to stroke her hair as I thought about Badb's promise to me, her love for my brother that would ensure we could pull this off. We *had* to.

"Don't worry, my love," I murmured gently. "I have a plan to save Asgard. If no one remembers us, if no one remembers my sword, Asgard will be spared."

Arnbjorg pulled away from me, staring so intently into my eyes I thought surely she could read my mind. And perhaps she could, because she slowly smiled and breathed, "Freyja."

So I slowly smiled back at her and confirmed her suspicion about who would help us save our world. "Freyja."

END OF BOOK THREE

Gavyn and Havard's stories come to an end in *Sword of Asgard*, the fourth book of the *Heroes of Asgard* series

ALSO BY S.M. SCHMITZ

Sign up for my mailing list, which will keep you up to date on new releases and great deals when I put books on sale, here.

For more information, please visit my website at smschmitz.com.

Other titles by S.M. Schmitz

Shadows of the Gods, book one of *The Unbreakable Sword* series (fantasy & mythology)

As a powerful demigod, Selena has been running from the gods who control the government agency, the New Pantheon, for the past three years, but now, they've caught up to her.

When they trap Selena in an alleyway in New Orleans, she is ready to admit defeat. But an unfamiliar demigod rescues her, and the more she learns about Cameron, the more she discovers their common bonds may be the key to unraveling her own mysterious history.

In the first book of The Unbreakable Sword series, Selena and Cameron must not only evade the New Pantheon, which is ruthlessly hunting the remaining gods and their descendants, but an angry Aztec god that wants Selena's power to himself. And they will discover in the impending final battle of the gods, no one can be trusted.

Blades of Ash, an *Unbreakable Sword* series prequel

When Olympus is destroyed, the Tuatha Dé and their Greek

**allies want revenge. But what their vengeance costs may
haunt them forever.**

Badb, one of the triune of Irish war goddesses known as the Mórrígna, is having a rough millennium: the mortals of Ireland have turned away from the Tuatha Dé, and now, the Sumerians have launched a disastrous invasion into Olympus.

Worse, the reason for the invasion isn't as straightforward as they first thought. With powerful players stoking the flames between the Irish alliance and their enemies, both sides may ultimately lose everything, including their own worlds.

The *Resurrected* trilogy, a science-fiction romance (also available in *The Complete Resurrected Trilogy Box Set*)

Awakened from death. Herself but no longer alone in her own body. Two lives merged into one.

A mistake. An aberration. A miracle.

And a company that wants her dead for existing.

When Dietrich's fiancée, Lottie, is killed in a car accident, he descends into his own personal Hell until he runs into her in a café two years later. Claiming she isn't really Lottie but only possesses some of her memories, the young woman offers him an unbelievable story then disappears.

Using his position as a CIA agent to track her down, Dietrich quickly discovers Lottie remembers far more about her past life than she'd originally let on. But his attempt to learn more about the planet she comes from or the woman she is now is disrupted by a group of men from the company that transports people from their home planet to Earth when they find out about her resurrection and attempt to murder her.

Because for Lottie, something went wrong, and her existence threatens their entire business on Earth. And Dietrich's ultimate second chance with the only woman he's ever loved will be threatened as well.

The Chosen, a *Resurrected* series novel

They promised her happily ever after. Instead, they gave her Hell. Now, she's getting revenge.

When Bella agreed to travel to Earth to start a new life with the man she loved, she'd been promised two things: healing dead human bodies so they could live on this planet always worked, and they could have the happily ever after forbidden to them at home.

But soon after arriving on her new planet, she discovers both of those promises were lies. And the consequences for trusting the wrong people are deadly.

After six years of hiding from the company that helped her cross over, she is approached by a beautiful but mysterious stranger who offers her a different kind of promise: the chance for revenge. And Bella's journey to end her own nightmare and to seek justice for the man she'd once loved is finally able to begin.

The Immortals series, a fantasy & mythology series (also available in *The Complete Immortals Series Box Set*)

When demons refuse to play by the rules, all Hell will break loose.

Colin and Anna have been hunting demons for a long time. But something is different in Baton Rouge. The rules are being broken and they're powerless against some of the greatest forces Hell can assemble. If they can't stop these demons from manipulating every rule of this war, then Heaven may lose the only battle that's ever really mattered.

The Golden Eagle, a romantic suspense

After a vicious second civil war in the U.S., the states that seceded are occupied, and the people there live by different rules.

Jon is the highest-ranking officer in an elite Task Force whose purpose is shrouded in mystery. Ava is just trying to survive the occupation after two years of brutal war. After meeting unexpectedly, they discover they are both willing to risk everything for the chance to love one another. But what those risks entail may be far greater than anything either could have imagined.

<u>*The Cambria Code*</u> series, a science-fiction romance

When a mysterious spaceship appears above Cambria, Zoe remains skeptical that it's anything but an elaborate hoax. By the time the first spaceship is joined by two others, Zoe reluctantly admits that Earth has been invaded, even though it's a pretty lame invasion: the aliens look remarkably human and keep to themselves. From what humans are able to learn about them, they seem incredibly arrogant and boring anyway.

After meeting Peyton, one of Earth's newest residents, Zoe feels an immediate attraction to him although she is reluctant to become involved with someone who isn't even human. But she soon discovers that these aliens are far more dangerous than they've led everyone to believe, and the secrets they are hiding may signal the destruction of her entire planet.

<u>*The Scavengers,*</u> a post-apocalyptic novella

When nothing is left, what will you treasure most?

In a world completely destroyed by adults, eleven-year-old Nic believes he is the only thing still alive after four years of isolation— the only thing except for the Scavengers.

When he meets Celia, another child in an empty world, they offer one another hope and the promise of an end to the kind of fear and loneliness that only a child abandoned on a dead and forsaken planet could understand.

But Nic's universe, for years centered around Celia, will be tested, and he'll discover just how far he's willing to go to protect them both.